Look for More Titles by Cassandra Chandler

PROGENITOR

The Forbidden Knights
FORBIDDEN INSTINCT

The Summer Park Psychics
WANDERING SOUL
WHISPERING HEARTS
LINGERING TOUCH
THE SUMMER PARK PSYCHICS OMNIBUS

Other Works
CRAFTING A WRITER'S LIFE: Building a Foundation

Coming Soon

Court of the Yuletide Fae
The White Stag
The Krampus

Cygnian 7
BRON
TARN
ROM

The Yule Cat

Court of the Yuletide Fae
Book One

Cassandra Chandler

Copyright Page

This book is pure fiction. All characters, places, names, and events are products of the author's imagination or used solely in a fictitious manner. Any resemblance to any people, places, things, or events that have ever existed or will ever exist is entirely coincidental.

The Yule Cat
Court of the Yuletide Fae, Book One
Copyright © 2022 by Cassandra Chandler
Print ISBN: 978-1-945702-13-6
Digital ISBN: 978-1-945702-12-9

First eBook edition: December 2022
First print edition: December 2022
10 9 8 7 6 5 4 3 2 1

cassandra-chandler.com
P.O. Box 91
Mission, Kansas 66201

Dedication

For Natalie Palma, who helped me rediscover the magic.

Don't miss out on any of the magic.
Subscribe to Cassandra Chandler's newsletter at
cassandra-chandler.com!

Chapter One

How did everything go so wrong?

The Yule Cat ran along the edge of a roof, calling to the wind to cover his tracks in the dense snow falling around him. The flakes stuck in his silver-white coat, obscuring the dark circles on his pelt. He had no tribute to bring to the Winter Queen. Not once had he returned without a new servant for her Court.

There would be a punishment. He would endure it, whatever it was, as long as she could help him purge this affliction in his chest. His heart was filled with… warmth. His fur stood on end as the skin beneath it crawled from the memory of the child's touch. She had hugged him. *Hugged* him—a fierce snow leopard twice her size with glowing blue eyes, fangs longer than her fingers, and gleaming mist trailing from his pelt.

That tiny mortal had thrown a blanket over his shoulders as if he needed her help. As if a mortal had anything to offer a mighty Fairy Lord, one of the only *two* in the Winter Queen's Yuletide Court. The child had wrapped her arms around him, wanting him to be warm, even though she had so little to warm herself.

The heat in his heart grew stronger, like a fire that had been lit within. A fire he didn't want any part of, didn't know what to do with. He was the Lord of the North Wind, icy and cruel. He tore warmth from others, leaving cold in its wake. He didn't accept it. He didn't *need* it for himself. He didn't want it.

Did he?

The Yule Cat let out a roar like thunder. Around him, the snowflakes shuddered, then paused, spinning in place as he pulled on the pocket of Faerie ruled by the Yuletide Fae. Light burst into being, a spiraling vortex of energy. He charged to the corner of the roof and leapt, arcing his back as he soared through the portal.

The light was so much colder than he remembered. On the other side, he landed in a drift, a shiver coursing through him as he shook his pelt free of moisture. His heat melted the snow clinging to his fur. The portal sealed behind him, the snap of its closure seeming to mark his failure complete.

An unfamiliar dread filled his stomach as he stalked toward the crystalline castle in the distance, rising from the snow and reflecting the verdant aurora flooding the dark sky overhead. When he reached the tall gates, they opened, motes of light threading through their faceted surface. Curious energy tickled his nose and tingled along his back, glowing lights of every color flying close and picking at his coat—pixies and sprites checking him over, as if the child he was supposed to have brought might be hiding in his fur. Their light caught in the hundreds of snowflakes slowly spinning, suspended in the air of the castle.

He hissed as he released his Yule Cat form. Silver magic enveloped him, lifting him to his hind legs. His pelt vanished into the light, replaced with rich sapphire blue silk that swirled around him as it coalesced into a loose shirt, dark indigo pants, and soft black boots that hugged his calves. He lifted his right arm in an arc, summoning the wind to form a silver cloak that swung itself onto his shoulders, anchoring in place with platinum clasps adorned with sapphires, diamonds, and blue topaz.

His heart was still warm. Disappointment surged through him, tightening his throat. He hadn't realized he held hope that his affliction would vanish along with his Yule Cat form. The pixies continued to pick at him, pulling on the ends of his cloak and tugging on his hair. They had never dared treat him that way before. A low growl built in his chest. He lashed out, summoning a harsh, cold wind to scatter them. The snowflakes hanging in the air spun more quickly as they fled. If only those pests were the worst he had to face.

The doors to the main hall stood open before him. He didn't dare hesitate and add showing fear to his shame. Puffing up his chest and drawing himself up ramrod straight, he strode into the chamber. The eyes of his Queen rested heavily on him as he walked to the center of the throne room and dropped to one knee, head bowed. At the edge of his vision, he could see the folds of her intricate dress, the fabric such a pale blue, it was almost white.

"You seem to be missing something, Lord North."

His spine prickled at the sound of his Queen's voice and the power laced through it. A power that was oddly muted. He forced a scowl to hide his surprise. It wasn't enough to conceal his turmoil. Before him, his Queen rose from her crystal throne. He kept his attention fixed to the floor.

"Missing something, but also… gifted something." She glided down the steps toward him, silent as a whisper. "Stand, Cat."

He felt the pluck of the command and his body jerked in response, but didn't rise. Panic flooded him, making the skin on his arms crawl again. A wind picked up in the room as if it wished to envelop him and carry him to safety. The Cat within him stirred, urging him to transform and flee. He could hide in the wintery countryside until he found a way to purge his affliction. His cloak stirred in the breeze and even the skirts of the Queen rippled.

He didn't need to see her face to sense her surprise. His powers had been summoned without conscious thought and dared to affect her. Worse, she had given him a command, and he hadn't obeyed. He didn't know how he had managed it, but he hadn't obeyed.

"Lord North," she said. Magic crackled through him as she summoned the bond of fealty through his name. His skin prickled as though he'd rolled in a patch of nettles in his two-legged form. "Stand."

She lifted her hand above him, power lashing out in tendrils of ice so cold they burned. He pushed himself to stand before her, but couldn't meet her scrutiny. She would see failure in his eyes—the mark the child had left.

"Where is your tribute?" the Winter Queen asked.

"I…" He shook his head. "I have none, Majesty."

"You are the Lord of the North Wind," she said. "The Yule Cat, feared by mortals."

"Not by her."

"Her?"

The word seemed to freeze the blood in his veins, the chill in the air making him shiver, yet, the warmth in his heart prevailed. It beat faster as he considered the danger he had placed the child in through his mistake.

"So, you do have a tribute," the Queen said. "You just *chose* not to bring her to me." The silence stretched on where he felt her intense focus on him heavily. After a time, she said, "Those who are unwanted in the mortal realm, those who are lost and need guidance, find purpose here. Is that not good enough for the child you chose as tribute?"

"My Queen—"

"Am I?" she broke in. "Look at me, North."

Once more, she used her voice of command, forcing his gaze to hers. He could scarcely breathe. His chest had surely turned to stone, his ribs crushing his heart. Her cold beauty crackled through him—skin white as snow, lips red as cranberries, eyes like green emeralds. The contours of her cheekbones were high and sharp, her features all sharp edged like the crystal around her. Like ice. A crown rested on her forehead, its platinum and diamond spikes rising up and contrasting with the pale hair pulled tight against her scalp, revealing her long neck.

He had always thought her beautiful. He had never thought her terrible. His skin crawled at the very idea of bringing the child he had selected as a tribute to this cold domain. The child who had somehow touched his heart with her warmth.

He had always thought the Yuletide Kingdom to be one of stark beauty and endless magic. Now, it looked to him like a wasteland of snow and ice. Unchanging. Unwelcoming. So unlike the child. North knew there was a part of the kingdom that was different—the only bastion of warmth in the realm. But as a subject of the Winter Queen, he would find no welcome there, either.

"I think perhaps you have another Queen," she said. Her attention dropped to his chest and her lips pulled into a frown. "Or at least, there is another who rules your heart."

"Majesty." A deep male voice met his ears.

"Ah, Lord Snow." The Winter Queen turned to greet the enormous man who approached them.

The Lord of Endless Snow towered over him, even though North was over six-feet tall himself. Snow's shoulders were twice as broad and he was packed with muscle. He wore all white—leggings and tunic, with a thick white fur tied at his shoulder and draped over one side. It was easy to see the monstrous Polar Bear lurking within the man before them and to understand the frightening stories of 'the Krampus' that mortals had woven around him.

"I trust your tribute is settling in," the Winter Queen said.

"I've taken him to the kitchens," Snow said. "He'll need a firm hand, but will serve you well in time."

"Excellent." She turned back to North, and said, "Our Lord North has returned alone, though I think he carries his tribute in his heart."

"What?" Snow leaned closer, bending down from his great height to peer into North's eyes. He sniffed loudly, then jerked back, blowing the air from his nose, rubbing at it. He shook his head sharply. "North, you reek of love. A mortal loves you."

"A child," North protested. "She thought I was her gift."

He snapped his mouth shut before more damning words could escape. Enough had already slipped out to deepen his shame. One of the Winter Queen's thin eyebrows rose and Snow crossed his arms over his massive chest.

"She thought the Yule Cat was a present?" Snow said. "The beast who comes on Christmas Eve to steal away children who don't receive new clothes?"

"I see." The Winter Queen smirked. "The little girl wanted a kitty. Does she think you're her pet now? Are you?"

"I am the Lord of the North Wind," North said, stepping closer. Snow darted forward to stand between them, sucking in a deep breath to make his chest even bigger. North lowered his head, trying to stop the growl that rumbled within him.

"Your temper has grown hot," the Winter Queen said. "We cannot have that in the Yuletide Kingdom."

"What are we to do about this?" Snow asked, his voice laced with concern.

"It's an affliction," North said. "Surely, there's something that can purge this warmth from me."

"It is not so easy to remove something that has found its way into your heart," she said. "No, it's much too late for that."

"Then what do I do?" North asked.

"You will return to the mortal realm and stay there until you have found a way to purge yourself of this... warmth," the Queen said with a slight shudder of distaste.

North was stunned. He couldn't believe what he had heard. Banished to the mortal realm? He had no idea how to undo what had been done. He could be stuck there forever.

"Majesty," Snow began. "Please, have mercy. North is…"

His voice trailed off as they stared at each other. North wasn't sure what Snow had been about to call him. Peer? Friend? Brother? The bond they shared was the closest thing to affection that North had known before this night. Now that he knew what true caring felt like, their partnership couldn't compare. Still, North's shame deepened as he realized that Snow would carry the burden of North's duties while he was gone.

The Winter Queen regarded North silently for a moment, then her lips pulled into a cold smile. North's heart pounded and his mouth went dry. His punishment was at hand. What could be worse than exile?

"Fine," the Winter Queen said. "You could not bring your tribute here as a servant, so you will bring her as your bride."

"What?" North recoiled. "She's a child."

He couldn't have heard the Queen correctly. This punishment was beyond anything he had expected. A mortal bride? His humiliation would be eternal.

"She will grow." The Queen shrugged. "When she has come of age, you will present her to me."

"But Majesty—" This time, it was Snow who protested. She silenced him with a sharp wave of her hand, holding her arm up before him.

"I don't know anything about winning a mortal's heart," North said.

"That is not my concern," she said. "If you can win her heart by Christmas day of her twenty-seventh year, I will forgive your failure tonight. If not…"

North's blood pounded in his ears loudly enough to nearly drown out her words.

"Your exile will be permanent," she said.

Chapter Two

Ice and snow managed to get into every slight gap in Melanie's clothes, chilling her neck and chest. The thick flakes swept into her eyes, half-blinding her. She was absolutely crazy to be doing this. Then again, she'd be crazy to let the opportunity pass. As long as the private baking lesson she had won didn't take too long, she'd be home in time for her own Christmas tradition—sitting by the tree at midnight as the Eve ticked over to the Day, waiting for someone who would never come. Who wasn't even real.

She probably shouldn't have gone ahead and dressed up for the occasion. Warmer pants would have been better. Or any pants, instead of a dress and woolen leggings. But it was Christmas Eve, and she always dressed to celebrate, even if she was spending this one with a complete stranger —at least the next few hours of it. How long did it take to bake a batch of cookies or whatever the owner of the Yuletide Bakery had in mind?

The storefronts on either side of the road were lit with gorgeous lights of every color. Fluffy flakes of snow caught the lights and glowed like a magical Faerie landscape. A pang threaded through her as she wished she could pause and enjoy it more, but frostbite was not on her agenda for the evening. The snow had driven everyone inside early, it seemed. She pulled the lapels of her dark blue peacoat closer to the silver-and-blue scarf she had knitted last year, then pulled the matching hat down farther over her ears.

Most of the buildings were dark inside, their owners at home celebrating with family. For once, Melanie didn't feel sad at the thought that she had none. She was too excited about what the evening held. She had taken a risk and shared something deeply personal in a writing contest and won first prize—an evening being tutored by the owner of the Yuletide Bakery. The bakery was in a cozy part of town she had somehow never explored. She had read up on it after winning the contest, and it sounded absolutely magical.

The owner's theme was "Christmas Year-Round." She loved that. Christmas was her favorite holiday, even if she spent it alone. She still went all-out decorating her apartment, hanging up lights, and dressing a beautiful tree. The tree was the most important part, because she always held out hope that one day, *he* would come back to her. She even hung a stocking for him filled with toys and treats—which was ridiculous on so many levels.

Melanie shook her head hard enough that snow

dislodged, sliding down her back and making her jump and squeal. It served her right. She'd made a promise to herself and was not about to break it. When faced with the choice of staying home alone and waiting for a fictional beast that she *had* to have imagined as a child to crawl out from under her tree or having a private baking lesson from one of the most successful bakery owners in town, she did the only sane thing.

Trudging out into the snow to spend an evening with a man I've never met in a place I've never been, knowing I'll then have to trudge back to my apartment in the middle of the night. Yeah. That's sane.

She scoffed at herself, but kept pressing onwards. Someday, she would have her own bakery. This was an amazing opportunity. A *real* opportunity. And she would still be home in time to wait by the tree. She walked faster, just in case.

Ahead of her, golden light spilled out onto the snow, cast from the plate glass windows of a storefront. It was bright enough to illuminate the street in front of it and somehow made the air seem warmer. A sign hung above the door, decorated with a flowing script that said, "Yuletide Bakery—Where Christmas is Eternal." Smiling despite the cold, she hurried forward to look inside.

Tables with the chairs stacked upside-down on top of them dotted the floor, letting her know it was a cafe as well as a bakery. The heavy-duty espresso makers along the far wall—brick with just the right amount of weathering—would have clued her in as well. In front of the coffee machines, glass display cases were filled with sparkling gold and silver lights that curled around empty trays. She wished she could have come earlier and seen them when they were full. There was still plenty to catch her eye.

Dark mahogany shelves lined the wall to the right of the display cases, adorned with ropes of evergreen and filled with books, mugs, and sculptures. A staircase wound around one corner, heading to a door on the second floor. Beneath it, a huge Christmas tree was nestled near a stone fireplace with a blazing fire within. Three stockings hung from the mantel, one green, one white, and one blue. The tree was covered in glittering silver and gold ornaments that complemented the lighting perfectly. She had never seen anything so beautiful, except maybe for her fictional childhood 'friend.'

Her breath caught as her gaze was drawn to movement right beneath the window. A man was stretched out on a window seat, his chest rising and falling with each slow breath. He was tall, his long legs crossed at the ankles, and his hands clasped over his stomach. His brown hair was long enough to dust his shoulders, with bangs that fell across his eyes. She wanted to run her fingertips over the dark stubble that dusted his strong jaw and trace his gorgeous lips, slightly parted in sleep.

Was *that* the owner? Her heartbeat spiked at the thought of spending Christmas Eve with the most beautiful man she'd ever seen, and her mind raced off with fantasies she should absolutely not entertain. He lifted his arm, crooking it so that he could rest his head on it. Blue-green eyes like arctic depths stared at her as his lips pulled into a smirk. For a second—only a second—she would have sworn his pupils were slitted. Like a cat's.

"The view is even better from inside," he said, his voice somewhat muted by the glass. "You coming in or would you rather stand out there and freeze to death?"

Her cheeks prickled with heat at being caught gawking at him, though she scowled at his teasing tone. Apparently, he was one of those guys who knew exactly how gorgeous he was. Good. That would make him less appealing.

She headed to the door. Snow was piled up in front of it. This might not have been as good an idea as she thought. Would she even be able to get home at the rate the snow was coming down? She wondered if he would let her sleep on the window seat if it came to that. Maybe stick around to keep her warm.

What the heck was she thinking? She shook her head again and pulled the door open. A blast of warmth and the most amazing scents wrapped around her the moment she did. Sweet cinnamon, earthy nutmeg, and the beautiful scent of chocolate and coffee overwhelmed her senses. She closed her eyes, taking a deep breath and savoring each smell, trying to sort them all out.

"Mind closing the door?"

She jumped at the man's voice so close. She hadn't heard him approach, his footsteps absolutely silent. He was even taller than she'd thought, and with her being shorter than average, that meant he towered over her. One long arm stretched above her and the other rested on the door jamb, boxing her in as he continued to smirk at her. She needed to duck around his side to enter the bakery, but took a deep breath and did so, pulling the door shut as she did.

He chuckled and turned to lock the door in one smooth movement. Why did he lock them in? It must be because the store was closed. She had been thorough in her research and knew that the bakery had held a contest like this every year for the last seven years. There had never been any complaints about him. Then again, with how gorgeous he was, a lot of people probably wouldn't mind his attention.

"Let me get your coat for you," he said.

She took off her hat and gloves and shook the snow from them, then tucked them into her coat pockets before unfastening the large black buttons. He watched each movement, his smirk firmly in place. His cocky attitude made her scowl deepen. Just because he was utterly gorgeous didn't mean she was going to throw herself at him.

Probably.

She stomped her feet on the carpet just inside the door to dislodge the last of the snow, then slid her coat off. He lifted it from her arms and hung it on a peg near the door. As he moved near her, the scent of cinnamon rolls flowed off of him. Her mouth started to water.

Definitely not throwing myself at the gorgeous bakery guy who smells like cinnamon rolls.

His shirt was a deep sapphire blue, unbuttoned enough to give her a tantalizing view of perfect collarbones and a glimpse of his smooth, muscular chest. She wanted to reach out and undo a few more buttons to see more of what was hiding beneath the soft silken fabric.

"It's Melanie, right?" he said, pulling her back from her fantasy. His voice had a nice, low timbre.

"Yes," she said. She waited a few moments for him to give her his name before giving up. "What do I call you?"

"North."

"North? That's it?"

"That's it." He shrugged, his smirk deepening. Was that a dimple? Oh crap, he had dimples. She had a weakness for those. And for strong hands with long, artistic fingers.

"You're chilled to the bone," he said. "The ovens will warm you right up."

Melanie balked as he gestured toward a door behind the counter next to the biggest display case. For some reason, images from fairytales she'd read as a child filled her head

—stories about children being popped into ovens.

She was being completely ridiculous. How was he supposed to give her a baking lesson without using ovens? She cast a nervous smile at him and nodded, then headed for the kitchen and whatever else the night held.

Chapter Three

This was the most delicious looking mortal North had ever seen. When Snow had insisted that North host a woman every Christmas Eve, trying desperately to find the bride that North had 'lost track of,' he hadn't been too keen on the idea. Snow thought it was because North didn't want to have to endure an evening with a mortal, but he had been living among them for two decades now. North had learned to appreciate the mortal realm and all it had to offer.

Spending his days sleeping in his apartment above the bakery while his employees ran around downstairs, using the night hours to make the most magical pastries in town, filling the place with warmth and sweet fragrances that lured in the most wary customer, had become his own private paradise. Over the years, he'd grown accustomed to the warmth in his heart. Liked it, even. He only had to make it through one more day without finding his bride and he could stay there forever. He had done everything he could to make sure that would happen.

Minutely studying the tasty morsel in front of him, a

shiver of doubt trailed down his spine. Her hair was too dark and straight. The child's had been curly and much paler. She had the same piercing eyes, though—blue as the ice in a glacier. It wasn't a common color, but that didn't have to mean anything. The woman, Melanie, was tiny. He had at least a foot on her in height. She wasn't wiry like most of the wealthy women who came into his bakery. No, Melanie had curves. Very ample curves. His height gave him a fantastic view of her cleavage.

He leaned over her to open the door to the kitchen when they reached it, indulging in another glimpse. Her skin was pale, but there was a flush of color around her collarbones, neck, and cheeks. It might be from the cold, but judging from the looks she kept casting his way, it might be from something else. His smirk deepened as she crossed into his kitchen.

"Oh wow…" she said.

The breathy sound to her voice hit him like a blow to the chest. He rubbed the spot, wondering what the hell that was. She spun in a circle, eyes wide and smiling lips somewhat parted. With a little distance between them, he could see that she wore a dress of deep blue with an ivy pattern woven onto the fabric in silver thread. The hairs on the back of his neck rose. Those were his colors. It had to be a coincidence that she was wearing them… Right?

Her pale eggshell-white leggings were tucked into dark blue boots trimmed with silver fur at the top. The dress hugged her waist, flaring out at her wide hips and plumping up those magnificent breasts. His jeans started to feel too tight as his cock stirred. Apparently, it didn't have the same misgivings he did.

"This is amazing," she said. "You even decorated your kitchen to look like Christmas."

He grunted an affirmative, trying to get himself under control. What the hell was wrong with him? His heart raced and his skin prickled with goosebumps. His fingers curled and uncurled, as if trying to summon her into their grip. Three minutes in her company, and he already wanted this woman as he'd never wanted someone before.

Another shiver of doubt coursed through him. Could she be the same person who had shown him his first kindness? His first taste of what it was to be loved? No, it couldn't be. This wasn't even the same town where she had lived.

He had settled on the other side of the continent—after visiting her foster family in his human form and ensuring the child would receive better treatment than the neglectful way they'd been raising her. He was certain after that conversation, she had enjoyed a much better childhood. He had made sure she would want for nothing, casting a gaes compulsion spell on her foster parents to care for her after giving them enough gems to provide for her. She would never have to work a day in her life, thanks to him. He just wanted her to live that life far from himself.

Keeping his distance was how North helped her. The Kingdom of the Yuletide Fae was no place for someone so warm and caring. At least, not in the Winter Queen's court. Once Christmas Day arrived, he wouldn't have to worry about returning—or condemning the child to an eternity of winter's cold. Perhaps, some day he would seek her out to thank her for how she'd changed his life. Some day *after* tomorrow.

"I can't believe I'm here." Melanie smiled at him, cherry-red lips beaming and sending another jolt through him. He wanted to taste them. To feel them on his body.

"Are you okay?" she asked, stepping closer. Again, his body tightened in response, his energy coiling as if waiting to wrap around her and pull her close.

"Yeah, I'm fine."

He needed to get the baking lesson over with and send her back to wherever she'd come from as quickly as possible. Luckily, he'd prepared all of the ingredients before she arrived. Everything was measured out in individual cruets and bowls, just waiting to be combined in the right order.

"This looks amazing," she said, surveying the table where the prep work had been laid out. "What would you like me to do first?"

His attention locked onto that tempting cleavage again and a whole slew of ideas flooded his mind. None of them had to do with baking, but a lot involved bending her over the table and exploring those lush curves. She stared up at him, her eyes bright with anticipation. Anticipation about *baking*. He needed to get his head in the game.

"I have some dough chilling in the fridge for my own take on Chocolate Crinkle Cookies," he said, rounding the table to stand beside her. "We can make a dough for Cocoon Crescents and start the Crinkles baking while the Crescents dough sets up in the fridge. It doesn't need to chill as long."

"Wow, sounds like you have this all sorted out."

He leaned a little closer. "I have done this a time or two."

She laughed and nodded. His heart gave a little skip at the sound. Laughter that sincere wasn't common. Damn, she was captivating. She reached into a pocket hidden in the full skirt of her dress, bringing his attention to how it ended just around her knees. It wouldn't get in the way if he lifted her up and pinned her against the wall…

"Shoot," she said. "I think I left my pen at home."

She pulled out a small, spiral bound notebook with a deep blue cover covered in a snowflake pattern from her pocket and flipped through it. He caught glimpses of pages filled with neat, flowery handwriting, but she turned them too fast for him to read. The strength of his curiosity about her surprised him. He wanted to know what was on those pages.

"You planning on stealing my secret recipes?" he

asked, his voice gruffer than he'd intended.

"No." She cast a teasing scowl at him that had him leaning closer again. "Your secrets are safe with me."

He felt another shiver at her phrasing. What were the odds that out of everyone in the world, on the final night before his exile became permanent, *she* would show up in his bakery? After he'd taken steps to make sure it never happened. He stared at her intently, trying to see a trace of the girl he had met. No, Melanie was too young to be the same person. She looked like she was just entering her twenties and that girl would be twenty-seven.

Melanie lifted her book and sort of waved it at him strangely, as if she were using it to pull something from him. "I won't steal your secrets, but before I leave tonight, I need to suck everything I can out of you."

He paused, angling his head to the side. The shiver from that statement was a hell of a lot nicer than the one before. Her face immediately turned scarlet. He could practically see steam coming off her cheeks and struggled not to laugh. His misgivings vanished in the heat brought on by her words.

"Learning," she quickly added. "I need to learn all I can."

"Sure," he said, not bothering to hide his smile.

"I wasn't going to write down ingredients or proportions or anything," she said, talking quickly and not making eye contact, "but I figure you have plenty to teach me. Like, for dough that needs to be chilled, how long do you leave it in the fridge?"

"Depends on the cookie." He rested his hand on the edge of the table, inching closer as he cast a charming smirk at her.

The flush darkening her cheeks spread over her chest as she smiled and glanced at him briefly. She was definitely interested, but this one... She would need to be warmed up if anything was going to happen between them, and he had to admit to himself that he was starting to really hope something would happen between them, even with his concerns.

The other women he'd entertained on previous Christmas Eves had all but thrown themselves at him. A couple literally had, pretending to trip and fall against him. He'd gotten rid of them as quickly as possible, as he had intended to do with Melanie. Now, though... Now, he wanted her to stick around. She fascinated him somehow. He just hoped that saying about curiosity and cats wouldn't apply to him.

"Oh, I found it!" She pulled a midnight blue pen from her pocket, her smile brightening the entire room. How could someone be so happy over a pen?

"You sure do love blue," he said.

"It's my favorite color."

She beamed at him with those ice-blue eyes. He couldn't stop himself from staring into them. Despite the color, there was so much warmth there—along with traces of that heat he was stirring up in her. Her smile faded and her lips parted. He could hear her heartbeat pick up as she leaned toward him. Maybe she didn't need as much coaxing as he thought. But then she sort of shook herself, pulling back.

"We should get started," she said, laughing nervously again.

"I suppose we should." He turned back to his prep work, quite a bit more keen on the evening than he had been before.

Chapter Four

Melanie was going to melt the dough at this point. They wouldn't need to preheat any ovens, North could just hand her the cookies, and they'd bake from the heat she was putting off from lusting after him. Even his name was sexy. The image of him placing cookies on her chest, then reaching down to pluck them off with his nibbling lips popped into her head.

She was being ludicrous. She would never do such a thing. It would make a mess of her dress. Not to mention that he was epically hot and probably wasn't interested in her. Plus, no one should eat raw cookie dough.

She glanced over at him as he started talking about the different ingredients in their little dishes, his profile just as striking as seeing him head-on. Who was she kidding? She would let him eat anything off of her that he wanted if he was interested.

Shaking her head again, she turned back to the ingredients, hoping to distract herself. She threw the softened butter into the stand mixer, then added the sugar and started it up to cream them together. When they seemed mixed enough, she added the vanilla and started on the other ingredients.

"Wait, I know what these are," she said. "These are Wedding Cookies."

"I prefer to call them Crescent Cookies."

"Aww, what's the matter?" she teased. "Are you afraid of commitment?"

Where the heck had that come from? Her cheeks prickled with heat again as she looked away, a stupid smile on her face that she couldn't get rid of. North leaned against the edge of the table and crossed his arms. The movement opened the collar of his shirt wider, letting her see more of his tantalizing chest.

"Right now, I'm more concerned about getting my recipes poached by a ringer," he said.

"What?"

Her eyes widened as she realized what she was doing. She was supposed to be getting a baking lesson from a master, and here she was, throwing his ingredients around and using his equipment without asking. She coughed a little to stifle the laugh that bubbled up at the thought of other 'equipment' she'd like to be using.

"I'm so sorry." She backed away from the mixer. "I didn't mean—"

"Relax," he said, following her retreat.

He told her to relax, but the way he moved and the intensity of his stare made her feel like he was about to serve her up instead of cookies. Not that she would even mind at this point. Except she would. Of course she would. It didn't matter how attractive he was, she didn't just hook up with strange men.

No, I sit in front of a Christmas tree every year by myself waiting for a magic cat to show up. That's so much healthier.

That was who she had been up to now, but this Christmas was different. She could feel it, ever since she won the contest—since she decided to make a change. How many more new things could she push herself to do? How many new tantalizing things could she let herself do if she got out of her own way?

"It's kind of a nice surprise to have someone with me in the kitchen who knows what they're doing." North leaned over her, his gaze dropping to her cleavage. "Most of the people who enter the contest seem more interested in tasting than baking."

She licked her lips reflexively and his eyes followed the movement. Her nerves flared up, the hair along her arms standing on end. Slowly, his smirk faded as his expression became filled with heat. His eyes almost seemed to glow. The light was familiar. Two bright spots of blue beneath her Christmas tree when she was a little girl. The eyes of the Yule Cat. She had thought he was the gift she had begged for and worked to earn for as long as she'd been with those foster parents.

All she had ever wanted was a cat to be her companion. The Yule Cat had seemed like something beyond her wildest childhood dream. She had lavished him with love when he'd crawled out from under the tree—an enormous snow leopard putting off a cold, white mist. At the time, she'd been young enough to believe in magic, and the experience had made it hard for her to stop, even when she was supposed to 'grow up' and move on from such things.

She had covered the Yule Cat with the blanket she brought down with her from her bed and wrapped her arms around him as much as she could to warm him, even though she herself was bitterly cold. He had felt so real, the softness of his fur, the rumbling growl that turned to a purr the more she promised to protect him, love him, and take care of him forever. Thinking about it now, it seemed insane. It always did, until she was sitting in front of her Christmas tree on Christmas Eve, wondering if there was any magic in the holiday that could bring her first friend back to her.

She'd researched the Yule Cat, and knew about the stories where he ate naughty children. The stories where he took children to Faerie were the ones she believed. Somehow, she knew that he had come to snatch her away from all the disappointments of her reality. Except he hadn't taken her. He had left her where she was, with foster parents who hadn't seemed to want her up to that point. If he really was the friend she had wished for, wouldn't he have come back for her by now?

Her foster parents had changed after that night. They were more attentive, but there was always a layer of fear beneath all their interactions. They had been so relieved when she moved to the other side of the country for college. Their behavior made it harder to believe the Yule Cat wasn't real. She had convinced herself that he had let her stay where she was to protect her, and had even intervened with her foster parents to make them be nicer to her.

She had watched for him under the Christmas tree every year since, just as she still planned to do tonight. She hadn't dressed up for North, she had dressed up for the Yule Cat. How pathetic was that? Now, she was standing in front of the most gorgeous man she'd ever seen, who inexplicably seemed interested in her, and thinking about how she needed to be home before midnight just in case this was the year that the Yule Cat returned for her to take her to a magical wonderland.

Unless she was done waiting. Unless it was finally time to move on and grab what was real and in front of her, even if it was only hers for a brief moment.

North didn't seem like the kind of guy to settle down. Why would he, as gorgeous and charming as he was? He gave off definite 'player' vibes. Maybe this once, she was ready to play.

He was still staring at her, very much like he wanted to

eat her up. She stepped forward, hoping he would do the same. His warmth seeped into her as he swayed in place, his gaze filled with uncertainty.

She took another step, closing the distance between them. He started to lean down when her stomach let out a huge growl. Her eyes widened as her hand flew to her abdomen, mortification chilling the heat from a moment before.

"I'm so sorry," she said. "I was in such a hurry, I think I might have forgotten to eat." She reached into her pocket and pulled out a granola bar.

"What the hell is that?" he said, his voice lower and rumblier than before.

"This? It's a granola bar."

"I know it's a—" He let out an exasperated gasp. "That's not dinner. That's… sawdust."

"It's good enough for now." She gestured to the stand mixer and said, "We have baking to do."

He made a disgusted snort, then turned around and flipped up the top of the mixer. After detaching the bowl quickly, he pulled out some plastic wrap and covered the dough. With his long legs, it only took him a few strides to reach one of the big fridges in the kitchen. He tossed the bowl inside and turned off the oven on his way back to her.

"What are you doing?" she asked.

"You're hungry."

She laughed, trying to hide her embarrassment. "I'm okay."

"I'm not. I can't have you being hungry and I sure as hell am not going to let you eat that dry piece of—" He took a deep breath and let it out slowly, visibly working to calm himself down. "I'm cooking you dinner."

Dinner? He cooked, too? And wanted to cook for her? Her stomach did a little flip, then let out another loud growl. She actually scowled at it, then turned her frown at him.

"That's too much to ask," she said. "It's okay, really."

"It's not okay and I don't recall you asking for anything. As a matter of fact, neither am I."

She wasn't sure what he meant by that until he ducked down, planting his shoulder against her hips, then stood, taking her with him. She ended up draped over one shoulder, feet and arms flailing on either side of him. Her face was just above his butt. The view was so good, some of the fight went out of her. She still shimmied in his grasp, prompting a swift swat to her rump.

She went still, and said, "Did you just *spank* me?" her voice incredulous.

"Stop wriggling."

Let's see how he likes it.

Impulsively, she reached out and swatted his butt. He stood straighter as he sucked in a quick breath. His grip on her waist tightened and he let out a sound that she swore sounded like a purring growl.

"Harder next time," he said.

Melanie let out an indignant gasp, even though her body had a very different reaction. Goosebumps raced across her skin as heat pooled in her belly. Her nipples hardened against the soft fabric of her dress and the firm muscle of his back. Her core pulsed with an ache she hadn't felt... ever.

"You're going to eat some real food, and that's final," he said.

She was so flustered, it took her a moment to respond. "Fine."

"Yeah, fine."

"But no more spanking."

Probably.

He made a disgruntled 'hmph' sound. She expected him to set her down, but instead he walked back into the main bakery area, then carried her up the staircase that wrapped around two of the brick walls. The view was dizzying, with all the lights and decorations, so she fixed her gaze on a single point—his butt. By the time he reached the second floor, her stomach was fluttering for a very different reason than the dizzying changes of view.

He opened a door and carried her into a darker section of the building. He paused and closed the door behind him, then toed off his shoes. His large palm cupped her calf. She gasped at the wave of heat that flooded through her from his touch. He ran his hand down her leg, pulling one boot and then the other from her feet before dropping them on the floor near the door.

"Granola bar," he murmured. "Like I would let you eat that crap in my bakery when I could make you some decent food."

Part of her screamed that she should be worried. This guy was manhandling her and carrying her to who-knew-where. He had even taken off some of her clothes—"*not nearly enough*" ran through her mind—and he hadn't even asked first. But a stronger part knew he would never hurt her. That he would take care of her and protect her. She had no idea where that belief was coming from, but it wasn't just her attraction to him.

There was goodness, familiarity, and yes, a whole lot of hotness in him. She could tell that this had the potential to be the start of the biggest adventure of her life. As he walked down the hall, deeper into what appeared to be his apartment above the bakery, she relaxed against him, eager to see what the rest of the night held in store.

Chapter Five

Had he gone crazy? What the hell was he doing, carrying this woman into his den?

I know just what I'm doing. I'm going to feed her, strip her, and spend the night exploring every inch of her body.

He shook off the image of them tangled in his sheets. No, he was just going to feed her, then finish the baking lesson and send her on her way. Into the dark, cold, snowy Christmas Eve night.

Yeah, like that's going to happen.

They passed through his living room on the way to his personal kitchen, soft Christmas music playing on speakers cleverly hidden near the ceilings. Another tree stood in the window, decorated with blue ribbons and silver lights—his colors from the Yuletide Kingdom. The fireplace sprang to life as he entered the room, motion sensors kicking in and turning on gas pipes that had the fake logs inside glowing in seconds. A large, comfortable couch sat in front of it. She could sleep there. Or she could take his bed and he'd sleep on the couch. Hell, he could transform and curl up on the huge, gray faux fur rug in front of his fireplace while she slept wherever she wanted.

Another image coalesced in his mind—of Melanie joining him by the fire and curling up against his back. That thought was even less welcome. It reminded him too much of the little girl who the Winter Queen had declared must become his bride. North didn't want a bride, he wanted a lifemate. And he would be the one to find her, to choose her. He wasn't about to let himself be forced to spend eternity with a woman that had been chosen for him by someone else.

Melanie... He could already see himself spending eternity with her. She had handled herself like a pro in his kitchen. Fit right in. And she was handling his 'enthusiasm' for feeding her better than he'd expected. Other women might have screamed for help or yelled at him to put them down or, hell, tried to cop a feel while his ass was right in reach. More than one of the women he'd had to spend Christmas Eve with had spent the night chasing him around the table instead of paying attention to what he was trying to teach them. He'd taken a few to bed, but sent them packing as soon as they were done. When he imagined being in bed with Melanie, the fantasy went all the way to waking up next to her in the morning.

This was dangerous. Not just how strongly he was drawn to her, but that it was happening on the last Christmas Eve that he needed to get through before the Winter Queen's edict ended. He should be hiding out in his bakery, not carrying around a soft, warm, lusciously-curved woman. Then again, if this was his last chance to enjoy a night with a mortal, he couldn't think of someone he'd rather be with than Melanie.

What if the Winter Queen somehow found his bride and summoned him back to Faerie forever? His odds would be worse if she set Snow after the bride. The Krampus was a fierce tracker and had never failed to find his target. But Snow had visited North frequently in the mortal realm to check up on him and had only asked about *North's* efforts in finding the woman. Snow hadn't mentioned going after the bride himself.

If North had met Melanie the next day, he wouldn't be so worried. They could take their time and explore each other and see if there was something between them without the specter of his Queen's gaes hanging over him. It wasn't just a command, but a spell that the Winter Queen had cast over him. He was bound to take his bride to Faerie—if he found her before the spell lapsed. He had only barely managed to evade the part of the spell that demanded he seek her out, using the contest and these Christmas Eves with mortal women to satisfy the essence of the spell while avoiding its purpose.

No, he *had* escaped. He had done everything right to keep the spell at bay. This would be the last night he would ever have to worry about returning to Faerie again. He was going to enjoy it, then see what his life had to offer when he was truly free.

He glanced over at Melanie's rump, her skirts bouncing as he walked. The sight made his mouth water. Her soft breasts pressed against his back and her shapely legs dangled in front of him. Taking off her boots had actually given him pleasure. The feel of her legs beneath his hands, the way her breath hitched at his touch, made him want to slide her down in front of him, tear off her clothes, press her against the wall, and bury himself deep within her. But he didn't want her distracted by hunger when he took her.

"Are you going to put me down now, or are you planning to cook with me draped over your shoulder like a Neanderthal?" Melanie's sharp voice brought him back to the room. They had reached the kitchen, and he was just standing there staring off at nothing.

He brought his free hand up to the back of her thigh— ostensibly to keep her steady as he let her slide down his front. Her scent exploded around him, honey-sweet with arousal. With the arm wrapped around her waist, he kept her as close as he could, so he could feel every inch of her pressed against him. He hissed in a breath through gritted teeth as her lush breasts rubbed against his chest. The fabric of her dress caught on his jeans and rode up her torso as she crossed his hips.

She quickly reached between them, smoothing down her skirts. They were standing so close that her arm brushed against the front of his jeans, torturing his rock-hard cock. He wanted her to open his pants and grab him. Maybe have an appetizer before he took her to his room. Her blue eyes were wide as she stared at him, lips parted as she gulped in air. Her chest rose and fell so quickly the movement caught his eye and kept it. He had followed her descent, bending his head close enough that he would barely have to shift forward to kiss her.

Her stomach growled again.

Dammit.

Her lips snapped shut and she stepped back, her blush deepening. "Sorry."

He should have let her eat the damn granola bar. But no, he wanted her well fed and ready for what he had planned. Now that he had made up his mind... It was going to be a long night.

"Don't worry about it." He felt his lips pull into a smile that bared his teeth.

Her eyes widened again as she stared at them, her brow furrowing slightly. She shook her head and turned around. Had she seen something that unsettled her? He ran his tongue over his teeth and found that his canines had sharpened without him realizing it nor willing it to happen. Melanie was bringing out the beast in him. He needed to be careful.

"How can I help?" She crossed to the stove, putting more distance between them. He stifled a growl. He wanted her close.

"No need," he said. He headed for the fridge and started pulling out ingredients, setting them on the counter.

"I *want* to help." She shifted closer, leaning against the counter. "I like to cook, too."

Warmth spread from his stomach up through his chest. If she was as good at the stove as the oven, this might really be something. He had never met anyone he wanted to share his love of everything kitchen-related with before. He pulled out a cutting board, one of his favorite knives, and set them up, then handed her a head of cabbage that he had washed earlier.

"Oh, fun," she said. "How do you want it?"

He wanted to lift her skirt and bend her over the counter. Then flip her back to face him and take her on the kitchen island. He wanted the damn food to be cooked so she could eat and he could move them on to dessert.

"Sliced?" She rolled the head of cabbage on the cutting board, staring at it intently. "Julienned?"

"Diced, actually. We only need a quarter of it."

"Interesting," she said, smiling over at him. She cut what she needed, then put the rest of it back in the bowl and handed it to him. He watched while she started to work, admiring her skill and precision. Damn, she did know how to cook. This was still going to take too long.

He rested his hand on the counter, pushing a bit of his magic out through the air of the kitchen. Everything would cook faster, taste better, and they'd be ready to eat in a fraction of the time. Melanie gave a little shudder as the magic-filled breeze swept past her.

"It's a little drafty." She glanced up at him briefly, smiling again. Her cheeks were still flushed.

"Let me help with that." He turned on the oven and the burner he planned to use, then reached up to grab his favorite skillet that hung from the high ceiling and set it on the stove to warm.

Melanie kept at her work. She fit right in next to him. Being with her was easy. That was new, too. The warmth in his chest flared again. At this rate, it wouldn't matter if he had to go back to the Yuletide realm. The moment he set foot in the place, he'd melt it and be sent right back to his beloved exile. With a chuckle, he turned back to the fridge to get the rest of what they needed.

Chapter Six

What was happening? Her baking lesson had transformed into the most romantic date she'd ever had. Not that it was a date. But it sure felt like one.

North's personal kitchen was as amazing as his professional one, just in a different way. The exterior walls were exposed brick and the interior painted a deep red that matched it. High above her head, every kind of pot, pan, or skillet she might ever need hung on racks mounted on the ceiling. Off to her right, another rack held wine glasses hanging above an impressive wine rack that was taller than she was. She would need a stepping stool to get anything down. Or, she could just ask North to give her a boost.

She imagined him lifting her, then wrapping her legs around his waist and grabbing his face for a long, deep kiss. Again, her skin erupted in goosebumps, fire blazing in her belly as her core ached. If she knew her stupid stomach wouldn't distract them with more growling, she would have pounced on him right then.

He put away the rest of the cabbage, then brought out a package wrapped in brown butcher paper. She still wasn't sure what they were having. After adding a tiny bit of oil to the skillet, he slid the meat from the package into it. The sizzle and pop made her mouth water even before the heavenly aroma reached her nose. Had he already seasoned it?

She glanced over and saw that it was already turning a nice brown. That was fast. He added some butter and diced onions, then reached for the cutting board with her cabbage. After she handed it to him, she carefully rinsed the amazing knife she had used and blotted it dry on a towel hanging near the sink. His smirk was closer to a smile when she looked back to him.

"What?" she asked.

"It's just nice to see that you know how to take care of a good knife."

Her stomach did a little dance at the compliment. "What else can I do?"

"How about you grab us a bottle of wine off the rack?"

"Sure." She crossed to the rack, staring at all the bottles, and wondering which to grab. Some of them looked really old. All of them looked expensive. "Which one?"

"Third row down from the left and two over. Grab some glasses while you're at it."

She counted out the rows and stacks and pulled out the bottle. The label had a polar bear on it along with dozens of snowflakes. She couldn't read the language. It didn't even look familiar. Stumped on that front, she glanced up at the wine glasses. Even if she jumped, she doubted she could touch them.

"Um, problem," she said, turning back to North.

He glanced up from the skillet and laughed. "Sorry about that. How about we switch?"

"Okay."

She hurried back to the stove. As they passed each other, their arms brushed, and more molten heat flooded her. She had never been so attracted to anyone nor had such chemistry. If she was imagining that he felt something similar toward her, she would be mortified. The lingering gaze he cast at her as he passed reassured her. She set down the bottle, then picked up the spoon he'd been using to stir the contents of the skillet. Her mouth watered at the aroma floating up from it as she set to work.

"This smells amazing." She was certain this was a stuffing for something. "What is it for?"

North placed a large cookie sheet that held several small squares of dough next to her. "Runzas."

"No way!" She looked up at him with a huge smile. "I've always wanted to try those."

He leaned a little closer, his warm breath fanning her face. "Well then, tonight's your lucky night."

She really, really hoped so. Her cheeks prickled and she felt the flush run down her neck and across her chest. His eyes followed, fixing on her breasts as an unmistakable heat sparked in his eyes. His lips looked soft. They were so close, she could rise on her tip-toes and kiss him if she wanted. Run her tongue along his mouth until he let her in. She would have to be careful of his teeth, though. His canines had looked wickedly sharp earlier. Almost as if—

She turned back to the skillet quickly, pushing the thought away. This was not the time for fantasies. There was a real, solid, gorgeous guy inches away from her and very obviously interested in something happening between them. She wouldn't mess this up.

"How about that wine?" she asked.

"Sure." He opened the bottle, chuckling as he did so. "I kind of feel like I should ID you."

Melanie snorted. "I get that a lot. I'm older than I look."

He paused turning to stare at her as his smile faded. "How old?"

"You're not supposed to ask," she said, casting a playfully disapproving frown his way. At least, she hoped she managed to pull that off.

He poured the wine and placed a glass next to her, but kept his distance. She wasn't sure if she'd offended him by not answering. Maybe he had a thing for young women and was afraid she was older than he wanted? She wasn't entirely sure she cared. She didn't want anything to ruin this evening. Besides, it was just one night. She never had to see him again after this if she didn't want to.

The thought felt like a weight in her heart. Not seeing him again after one Christmas Eve wasn't what she wanted. But she had thought her loneliness was over before, or at least, she had dreamed that it had been. The Yule Cat had left her. Would North do the same?

"You're letting the meat get a little scorched there," he said.

"Oh, sorry." She scraped at the skillet, loosening the bits that had become stuck. It didn't seem too crispy, thankfully.

North came to stand behind her, his arms wrapping around hers as he covered her hands with his. "You need to ease into it."

His chest was flush against her back, his hips pressed against her backside. She closed her eyes and leaned into him, feeling him enveloping her. He nuzzled her hair, his breath causing it to tickle her neck. The scent of pine wrapped around her, mingling with the amazing aroma from the food. If her stomach growled again, she was going to… To do something to it.

"That looks about ready to me," he murmured against her ear, his voice low and provocative.

"Yeah." Shivers ran all along her arms at his closeness. She wished she hadn't worn a long-sleeved dress. Or any dress.

"Why don't you let me take over?" He took the spoon from her, turning her toward the counter. "Get yourself some wine."

She nodded, heading straight for the glass filled with dark red liquid. His was already almost empty. She took a sip and flavor exploded on her tongue. It was as if she was drinking a molten cherry cordial, but without being cloyingly sweet or thick. She took a deeper drink, shivering as the wine burned its way down her throat to her stomach.

"Go easy on that, now," he said. "At least until you've had something to eat in you."

She turned back to him, wishing she had the guts to make a quip about what she wanted in her, but only let out a little choked noise. The runzas were already filled, formed, and coated in a light egg wash.

"How…" She pointed at the tray. "Don't those need to rise again?"

"Not the way I do it."

Warmth rolled through the kitchen as he opened the oven door. He lifted the cookie sheet and placed it inside, then sealed them in and set a timer. Wiping his hands on a towel, he approached her, caging her body against the counter with his. If she wanted to, she would barely have to move to touch him. And she really, really wanted to. She wanted *him*—more than she'd ever wanted anyone. He set down the towel next to her and kept his hand there, using his free hand to take her wine glass and set it aside.

"Besides," he said, leaning close, "things don't take

long to rise again around here."

She started to laugh at the cheesy line, but then he suddenly leaned forward, capturing her lips with his. Everything within her felt as though it had caught fire. Her abdomen filled with heat, burning through every thought until all she had left was need. His hands gripped her hips, lifting her easily onto the counter. She wrapped her legs around his waist, pulling their hips together. With a groan, he ground his erection against her, his tongue plundering her mouth. He tasted of the sweet cherry wine.

His hands kneaded the soft flesh of her backside, encouraging her to move against him. He hooked his fingers in the top of her stockings, lifting her briefly to pull them down. The cool air hit her bared flesh, that breeze flowing over her most sensitive skin in a tantalizing wave. North grabbed her thigh and pulled it from him, keeping his chest clamped to hers as he tugged her stockings from that leg. He lifted her back in place then tugged her stocking from the other leg. His jeans chafed against her thighs as he thrust against her, but she didn't care.

He kissed his way to her neck, his nails tracing her scalp as he grabbed her hair and tilted her head to the side. Her skin rose in goosebumps, her nipples tightening as her core pulsed. He raked his teeth over her skin as he dragged his hand along her breast. He hefted its weight, groaning against her as he squeezed it. The hand at her backside vanished briefly as he shifted his hips from hers. She heard the distinct sound of a zipper being pulled.

Were they really going to do this here? Now?

The tip of his shaft pressed against her heated flesh, his hand returning to her backside as he slid her closer to the edge of the counter.

Yeah, they were doing this now.

She tightened her legs around his waist, pulling him closer, gasping as the velvet skin of his crown parted her flesh. He grunted, his grip on her hair tightening and his nails tracing her scalp again. Jolts of pleasure raced along her spine and back. He pressed deeper, stretching her, then backed away, rocking slowly to let her body get used to his size. Her core throbbed with an aching need. She needed him deeper, faster. She needed *him*.

"North," she gasped, tightening her legs around his waist further and angling her hips against his. "Please."

His hand on her backside twitched, then in one fluid movement, he lifted her and pulled her forward, driving himself deep within her. She cried out as suddenly she was so full, his cock stretching her beyond any limits she'd known. He released her hair and brought both hands to her hips, holding her against him and not moving aside from his panting breath. Energy coiled inside him. She could feel it. The desperate need to move, but he was holding himself back for her, letting her adjust before proceeding.

She put her hands on his shoulders as the throbbing ache turned into more of that molten heat, her body burning with it. Pressing against him, she lifted herself along his shaft, every inch of friction tightening her body with need. She pulled him to her, kissing him deeply, exploring his mouth like he had hers earlier, rocking against him as she urged him to give in to his own need. His fingers tightened on her again, lifting her higher, then letting her plunge back down, impaling her on his shaft. Over and over again, he thrust into her, pushing her closer to bliss.

"North," she gasped. "More."

He set her back on the counter's edge, bracing her with his hands. Each thrust grew more urgent, his hips moving faster, his cock landing deeper. She locked her ankles behind his back, letting go as he rode her hard. Pressure built deep in her belly, her skin was on fire everywhere they touched while that coolness in the air caressed where they didn't. The contrast pushed her higher, the pleasure rising until it exploded along every nerve in her body.

She threw her head back and screamed his name as his thrusts became frenzied, her core pulsing as his movements prolonged her own release. His fingers dug into her flesh almost painfully, keeping her steady as he rammed himself into her over and over again. He buried his face in her neck as he let out a pleasure-filled groan, his cock throbbing deep within her as he released his seed. He kept himself pressed deep, nuzzling her neck as their bodies vibrated with the last echoes of their pleasure.

"Woman," he murmured against her neck. "You are going to ruin me."

Chapter Seven

His woman was still hungry, but North was starving. Not for food, but for more of her body. More of the amazing pleasure she had given him. He forced himself to pull away from her, but left his pants open. He was going to be buried inside of her again as soon as possible and didn't want anything in their way.

The runzas had to be done. He turned to the oven and opened it, barely remembering in time that he needed to use a hot pad when mortals were present. He pulled out the tray and set it on top of the stove, then leaned forward and blew on them, his head angled away so that she couldn't see what he was doing. A little bit of the North Wind's chill, and these would be ready to eat immediately.

He stepped back and gestured to them. "Eat. Quickly."

She blinked heavy-lidded eyes, then laughed. "I'll burn my face off."

"It's okay." He picked one up and took a big bite. The flavors had turned out better than he had hoped. As soon as he managed to swallow, he held another up to her lips. "A drafty kitchen is good for cooling things off."

He doubted even the full freezing power of the North Wind could help him, though, especially when she licked her lips, then leaned forward to take a bite of the runza he held up for her. He groaned inwardly as her eyes rolled shut. Stepping closer, he fed her another bite, then another, savoring the movement of her lips and each sound of pleasure.

"Oh my God," she said. "These are so good."

He handed her another, then finished his own in one bite. How many would she need to be full? He snatched another for himself, eating it as quickly as he could. When he turned back to her, she was sitting with her eyes closed, cradling the half-eaten runza near her nose. She let out a contented sigh, lost in his cooking. His chest tightened. Cooking for others had always pleased him, but he had never enjoyed such happiness while watching someone enjoy his food—not even previous lovers.

Could he call them that? Lovers? After being with Melanie, he wasn't sure. 'Hook-ups' seemed more appropriate for what he'd experienced before this. Brief shared physical pleasure, then moving on with his life.

He didn't want to think about moving on beyond Melanie. He didn't mind thinking about moving up behind her. If she stood in front of the counter, he could reach up and lift her breasts from their bodice, cupping them as he rammed into her. His cock began to stir, straining toward her.

"Melanie," he said, taking a step toward her.

She opened her eyes, her soft smile gutting him. He wanted to drop to his knees and ask her to stay with him forever. That would be certain to scare her off. It was too soon, for her at least. Mortals needed time to accept their emotions. Immortals... not so much. In that moment, North knew that she was his. Forever.

Her eyes traveled down his body, widening as they reached his cock. Her mouth dropped open, and a whole new set of fantasies paraded through his mind. She could slide from the counter to her knees and take him in her mouth while he fisted her hair and encouraged her movements. Or, just lift her onto the kitchen island. He kept it clear, so they wouldn't even knock anything to the floor, though that held its own appeal.

"Do you need more?" he asked.

She nodded, leaning back, and bracing her arms against the counter.

He chuckled and said, "I meant the food. Are you still hungry?"

"Not... Not for that."

Thank the Gods.

He practically leapt forward, grabbing and kissing her again. She clasped his arms, meeting his kiss with equal passion. He reached between them and tugged on the fabric of her dress, undoing a few buttons so that he could lift her breasts. She gasped as the cool air of the room hit them. He leaned back, desperate to see, to taste, to experience all of her.

The soft weight of her breasts in his hands sent a thrum of pleasure to his cock. Bending down, he lifted one to his mouth, sucking on the stiff peak of her nipple, flicking it with his tongue until she was writhing before him. He shifted his attention to the other, kneading the first and running his thumb over the taut bud. She was groaning when he finished, eyes pinched shut and breath coming fast.

He pulled her forward off the counter, holding her up as she landed on her feet and diving in for a deep kiss. She buried her fingers in his hair, clawing at him as if she were as desperate for him as she was for her. Surely, that wasn't possible. He wanted her with an all-consuming fire that threatened to melt his world. She lifted her leg along his thigh, letting out a whimper as he pinched and rolled her nipple between his thumb and forefinger.

It was more than he could take. With a growl, he released her, spinning her around to face the counter. He grabbed her hands and planted them where he wanted them on the counter, then gripped her hips and lifted her, lining up his shaft with her core. Without hesitating, he buried himself to the hilt. She cried out, fingers curling against the counter. His thrusts shoved her forward with each stroke. He leaned over her, plastering his chest to her back, and embraced her, grasping her breasts to continue his pleasurable torment.

She was so tight and wet, her heat seeping into him. He needed more. His chest was so full of need, he thought it would burst. Each stroke sent his heartbeat racing faster. He dropped one hand to the folds of her dress, lifting her skirts until he could reach the apex of her slit.

She groaned as he found her nub and circled it with his fingers, bending to suck and nip her earlobe as he did, never letting up with his attention to her breasts with his other hand, pounding into her, forcing her body to take every ounce of pleasure he could give her. He felt her coil, her body stiffening, then she cried out his name, her voice even louder than before. He pounded into her faster, pushing her into the highest ecstasy that he could, only slowing when she slumped against the counter before them.

"God, North," she said. "You've already ruined me."

He gently bit the shell of her ear and whispered, "I'm just getting started."

He pulled himself from her, though his cock protested, throbbing against the cold air. He spun her around, capturing her mouth in a deep, claiming kiss. Lifting her again, he set her on the island, then slid her farther from the edge, climbing after her. He pushed her onto her back, spreading himself over her body, pulling her thigh up so that he could slide deep into the bliss of her core. Her back arched and her head thrashed as new pleasure racked through her.

Each thrust landed harder, her core pulling at him, urging him to his own release. He propped himself on one arm to use the other to grip her breast and knead it, his hips rocking against hers. Claiming her lips again, he thrust his tongue deep, dominating her mouth, their breaths mingling as his magic swirled around and through them. Pressure built deep in his gut, his cock throbbing with the aching need to fill her again and again. He ground against her clit each time he landed in her, pushing her to her own pleasure.

Releasing her lips, he nuzzled her ear, cock throbbing, body taut, then said, "Come with me, Melanie."

"Yes," she murmured back. "Yes!"

He slammed deeper as his cock exploded into her. She arced her hips to meet each thrust, writhing beneath him as her pleasure suffused her. Each pulse of seed resonated through his entire body until he was thrumming with pleasure. Her core pulsed around him, pulling everything he had to give. Breathless, he half-collapsed on top of her, barely keeping his weight from her.

"You are mine," he said.

She swallowed hard, then traced her hands along his back and pulled him closer into her embrace.

"Only if you're mine, too."

Chapter Eight

Melanie wasn't sure when they made it to the bed. It was sometime after the couch, the shower, the rug in front of the fire, and back in the kitchen during a midnight snack. Christmas Eve had come and gone, and it was Christmas Day—the first Christmas Day that she wasn't spending alone since she'd left her foster parents' house. She stretched out along North's warm body, feeling his latest erection prodding her backside. That was not something she wanted to let go to waste.

She half-sat up as she started to roll over, but then yelped, pulling the covers up to her collarbones. An enormous man was standing at the foot of the bed. His dark hair was cropped close to his scalp, shorter than the stubble on his wide jaw. His arms were crossed over the biggest chest she'd ever seen. He must be seven feet tall at least and was packed with muscle that strained against the fabric of his clothing. He was dressed in a white uniform with gold and red trim that looked like something a fairytale prince would wear. A cape of thick white fur was slung over one shoulder. His eyes were such a warm brown, they almost looked red as well. It had to be a trick of the light.

He cast an oddly familiar smirk at her and said, "Good morning."

Melanie reached over and grabbed North's shoulder, shaking him hard. He mumbled something incoherent, then wrapped his arms around her waist, pulling her closer.

"Stop that," she hissed. "Someone is in the room with us."

"What?" North blinked sleepily and let out a huge yawn.

"Damn, North," the stranger said. "Did you guys bother to get any sleep last night?"

North's eyes widened as he bolted upright. "Krampus? What are you doing here?"

At least they knew each other. Melanie's apprehension lessened a tiny amount. It was still weird that this guy thought he could just walk into North's bedroom and—

"Wait, did you say *Krampus*?" she asked.

"You can call me Snow, if you'd rather," the giant man said.

"Snow," she repeated.

He shrugged, that infuriatingly cocky smirk deepening. It was just like North's, only where North exuded swagger, this guy had a quiet confidence that scared the crap out of her. There was no doubt this guy was the toughest person in the room, and he was absolutely aware of it. Heck, he was the toughest person she'd ever seen.

"Time to go," Snow said. "Come on, the Queen is waiting. You've left your duties for too long."

"Queen?" Melanie looked back at North. His face was drawn and pale, his lips pressed in a thin line. The newcomer was dressed like a prince. Did that mean… "Are you royalty or something?" she asked.

"Or something—and not anymore." He wouldn't look at her as he spoke. With a broad gesture to Snow, North said, "It's Christmas Day and I missed the deadline. My exile is permanent now."

"Exile?" Melanie said. "North, what is going on?"

Finally, he turned to her, shaking his head. He took her hand in his and said, "Nothing. Nothing you need to worry about."

"'Nothing.'" Snow snorted, then laughed. "Sure. There's nothing anybody needs to worry about because everything is taken care of now." He inclined his head toward Melanie and said, "Merry Christmas, by the way."

"Merry… Christmas." She half-smiled as she turned back to North, trying to find a clue to what was going on in his expression. She'd be a lot less nervous if he didn't look so upset. And if she had clothes on.

"Come on." Snow clapped his massive hands together. "Time to go."

"We're not going anywhere," North said though gritted teeth.

"Of course, we are." Snow chuckled again. "Now get moving." He reached for the blanket and tugged on it.

"Hey!" Melanie slid off the side of the bed to her feet, dragging the covers with her. She glanced back at North, who was just crouched on the bed, staring at Snow as if he were about to pounce on the huge man. Naked. She had to help him.

"We're not going anywhere," she parroted.

"Not like that you aren't." Snow lifted one massive leg and stomped it on the floor hard enough to make the pictures on the walls shake. A glowing snowflake appeared under his boot. With the sound of crackling ice, more snowflakes formed, darting toward her over the dark hardwood floor in a line that extended from his foot.

Melanie yelped again, jumping back as the snow reached her feet. It spread so quickly, there was nowhere she could go to escape it.

"Hey!" North leapt from the bed, landing in front of her, but the snow already had her in its grip.

Aching cold spread up her legs and body, coating her in the feeling of pins-and-needles. The crackling turned into the swishing of fabric as the snow covered her body, coalescing into a velvet and silk dress in deep sapphire blue with intricate silver embroidery. The smooth skirts plumped around her legs as she felt a petticoat form underneath it, and the bodice laced up snug along her ribs, lifting her breasts in the perfect décolletage. The sleeves were tight along her upper arms, then flared out along her forearms and wrists.

Ice wound around her fingers, solidifying into rings of white gold with channel set sapphires. More crept along her neck and up through her hair, lifting it from her neck. She shivered as the cold ran along her scalp, pulling her hair into a chignon. A heavy weight settled just above her breasts and she glanced down to see a huge sapphire surrounded by diamonds and suspended by a gorgeous platinum chain around her neck.

Her freezing feet were wrapped in warm boots that lifted her slightly as heels extended from their soles and stockings snugged against her legs. A whirlwind of snow swept over and around her, then suddenly dropped to the floor, and vanished. She gaped up at Snow to see his arm stretched toward her, his fingers splayed wide. His lips pulled into a huge smile.

"So?" He dropped his arm to his side as he looked at North. "What do you think?"

Melanie thought she might be having a mental breakdown. She dropped the covers she'd been holding onto so she could fully see the gorgeous gown she was draped in, then lifted her hands to look at the jewelry on her fingers. She briefly lifted the skirt's hem to study the dark blue, soft leather boots peeking from under her skirts. It all felt so real.

Just like the night when the Yule Cat had visited her.

"What is happening?" she said, her voice a tight whisper.

"Dammit, Snow," North said. "Leave her be."

"I can't do that." Snow shook his head. "I have orders to take you both back to the Yuletide Kingdom. It's time for you to come home."

Chapter Nine

This was a nightmare—worse than a nightmare because it was actually happening, and because Melanie was caught up in it with him. Was Snow willing to take whatever woman North had slept with on the last Christmas Eve of his exile back to the Winter Queen and just say that she was his bride? The Queen would see through any ruse they tried. She would know that Melanie wasn't the girl that had sparked warmth in his heart all those years ago. But the Queen might decide to keep Melanie as a servant, the very fate that North had tried to avoid for the girl who had given him his first glimpse of love and caring.

"She's not my bride," North said.

Snow laughed. "Of course, she is. Don't be stupid."

North stood, working his own magic to conjure clothing around himself—the dark blue button-up shirt and jeans he preferred. Melanie made a little choked gasp. Her eyes were wide enough to show the whites all around their irises. His heart tightened at the thought that this was driving her away from him. Surely it had to.

"How did you do that?" she asked, her voice quavering.

"I can explain." North knew he was stalling. He had no idea what to tell her or how she would react. They hadn't known each other long enough for him to have time to even consider telling her about him. He didn't know what to say or do. He reached for her and she jerked back. The movement felt like she'd stabbed him through the heart with ice.

"You can figure this out later," Snow said. "I know you've been dicking around in the mortal realm for a long time, but some of us still have responsibilities. I'm on a schedule and you're underdressed."

Once more, Snow thumped his foot on the floor. The snowflake pattern darted toward North, then swirled up his legs and torso and flowed down his arms. He was left in indigo velvet breeches and a sapphire jacket with two rows of dark blue buttons running straight up along his torso in formal rows. Snow had even pulled North's hair back with a tie.

"How did you do that?" Melanie nearly shouted, this time at Snow. At least she wasn't cringing as much as she had been. A bit of hope sparked in North. Maybe he could salvage this after all. "And what do you mean, 'mortal realm?'"

Then again, maybe not.

"This is all just a misunderstanding," North said. He took a step closer to Melanie, and this time, she didn't back away. "Don't worry, I won't let him take you anywhere."

"What did I just say about being stupid?" Snow laughed and shook his head, but the skin at the corners of his eyes tightened.

North knew his friend well enough to see the signs of his patience fraying. 'Let sleeping bears lie' was an understatement when it came to Snow. He put both hands on his hips and took a deep breath, his scrutiny intensifying as he stared at North.

"You are both going to appear before the Winter Queen." Snow's words were carefully measured as he spoke, and utterly calm, which was more unnerving than anything else he'd done. "Are you coming with me or am I *taking* you there?"

"Snow, please," North said.

"What is wrong with you?" Snow shook his head. "You should be thrilled to be coming home—and bringing your bride with you."

"I can't go back there and I sure as hell am not taking Melanie." North took a step closer, his voice pleading. "The Yuletide kingdom has become locked in a joyless, unchanging winter since the Queen established her own domain. Don't you remember the colors of autumn? The warmth of summer or the flowers of spring?"

Snow snorted. "I'm the Lord of Endless Snow. What do I care about spring? I'll tell you what I do remember. I remember that I can kick your ass and that your time is up."

Snow took in another huge breath. As he did, a whirlwind of snow flew up around him, coating his body in bright white light. North knew what was coming. If he could distract Snow long enough, maybe Melanie could escape. It didn't matter what dreams North had dared to entertain about her. He wouldn't condemn her to an eternity in an icy wilderness just because Snow was intent on bringing North back with a 'bride.'

He turned to Melanie, and said, "As soon as you can, run."

"What? No." She shook her head sharply, concern etched in her expression—not for herself, but for him.

In that moment, North knew that his heart was forever lost. He would do anything to protect Melanie—even if it meant losing her.

"I won't leave you," she said.

His chest constricted, his heart was shattering like a fallen icicle. He knew how she would most likely react when she saw him transform. Mortals didn't adjust well to their first view of magic.

"You will," he said.

He turned back to Snow, readying himself for a battle he knew he couldn't win. Snow wasn't boasting when he said he could kick North's ass. North was smaller, more agile, and definitely faster. He could keep Snow busy while Melanie escaped.

Snow's face elongated as his skin turned as white as his namesake, fur began sprouting everywhere. His fingers curved into huge clawed paws, his nose darkened to black, and his ears pulled up into round crescents on either side of his head.

North didn't wait for him to fully transform into his polar bear form. Coiling, North pulled forth his Yule Cat form. Silver fur with black spots sprang from his skin as a whirl of light enveloped him. His teeth lengthened as well as his ears, his face pushing forward into a muzzle. His claws gripped the crumpled blankets Melanie had dropped on the floor, their shared scent blooming around him as his senses intensified.

A shrill screech jolted through his heightened hearing, throwing him off balance. He hissed in response, turning toward the source of the sound. Melanie had pressed herself against the wall, eyes wide with terror as she gaped at Snow. It wasn't enough that he was fully transformed into his polar bear form. Mist and snowflakes swirled around him, sending a chill through the air that made even North shiver. Snow covered his ears with his paws, the mist and snow dissipating as he shrank back to his human form.

"Gods, is she always this loud?" he said, still covering his ears with his hands.

This was North's chance. He wouldn't have a better

one. He coiled his body, preparing to leap as Melanie's scream suddenly cut off. The change was so abrupt that he turned to her, ears perked forward. Her eyes were still wide, but instead of fear, shock and confusion flooded her features. She took a step closer, than another. How could she not be afraid of him?

"You," she said, lifting a trembling hand toward him. She shook her head suddenly and pulled back. "This isn't happening. This can't be real."

"You know it is," Snow said. "You studied the lore in college."

"How…" She swallowed hard, her focus riveted on North, though her head angled toward Snow. "How do you know what I studied in college?"

North wanted to hear the answer as well. His stomach tightened as foreboding swept through him.

Snow arched an eyebrow and grinned. "Who do you think paid for it?"

"I got… a scholarship," she said, haltingly.

"That you won because of your essay on 'The Night I Met the Yule Cat.'" He made air quotes as he said the last bit.

North's heart started to pound. Melanie couldn't be… Could she?

"I had my subjects go through most of the submissions after telling them what to watch for," Snow said. "Finalists from all over the world were invited here, to North's town, for a full-ride scholarships plus room and board at the local university—provided they study folklore. You'd be surprised how many that weeded out. I figured you would stick around after school. Then I just needed to get you and North in the same room to let the magic take its course. Hence the 'My Most Magical Christmas Eve' contest that you won this year."

"No," Melanie said, shaking her head.

"You sure as hell didn't make any of this easy." Snow turned to North and said, "Either of you."

"This isn't possible," Melanie said. "It can't be real."

Snow laughed. "It's right in front of you. The Yule Cat. *Your* Yule Cat. And you are his bride."

Melanie backed away from them both. The turmoil in her eyes tugged at North's soul. Was she really that same person he had met and spared so long ago? The girl who had first shown him kindness?

If she was… their fates were sealed.

Chapter Ten

There had to be an explanation for this. People didn't just turn into gigantic polar bears and then back again like it was no big deal. They didn't turn into… into… Melanie swallowed past the lump in her throat, her eyes still locked on the snow leopard crouched in the blankets at her feet. He stared back at her with blue eyes that were so familiar. North's eyes. And earlier…

The Yule Cat.

Her ribs ached from the punishing beat of her racing heart—and more, from the fact that he had left her. Now he was sitting in front of her as if nothing had happened. As if he hadn't left her alone all those years, questioning her sanity, questioning her worth. Why had he left her behind?

"You can't be here." She pointed at him as her voice grew more shrill. "It's not right. Not now. Not right when I decided to stop waiting by the Christmas tree for you every year. Not when I finally realized it wasn't worth it."

The Yule Cat—North—flinched, a low hiss escaping his muzzle. He lowered his head and backed away.

"Don't you dare run away from me again," she screamed, her eyes burning with tears. Her entire body began to shake as rage and the shock of seeing him took hold. She took a step after him as he retreated. "You left me. You *left* me. You were supposed to be mine. I wasn't going to be alone anymore. But you made me more alone than I had ever been."

Light swirled around North. He rose on his back legs, his fur retreating into his skin and his face reverting to the human features she had lovingly traced with her fingertips and lips just hours before. His eyebrows were knitted together, the skin around his lips pulled tight in despair.

"I'm so sorry, Melanie," he said.

"For what?" She scoffed. "For freaking me out with your giant bear friend? Or not telling me that you're a shapeshifting Yule Cat? Or for leaving me on my own to wonder if I was crazy for most of my life?" She took a step closer and jabbed her finger against the hard muscles of his chest at the last question. "Or the worst of it—giving me a glimpse of a magical world just beyond my reach, one that I had dreamt about and longed for, and then leaving me here with nothing and no one."

"I didn't leave you with nothing," he said. "I gave your foster parents money. I ordered them to take care of you."

She snapped her mouth into a tight line. So much made sense now. Before that night, her foster family had always seemed to have enough, though her foster parents hadn't really shared much with Melanie beyond what was expected. After the Yule Cat came to her, they had showered her with gifts, clothes, and toys. They had also been even more stand-offish than before. They had taken care of her, but not cared for her. Now, she realized they must have been terrified. She had no doubt that North had used his magic to convince them to become 'better parents.'

"I was still alone," she said. "More than ever because I knew no one else had experienced anything like the things that I had. I couldn't talk to people about it without sounding crazy."

"Melanie—" North stepped forward, reaching for her. She jerked back reflexively. It would be too easy to give in if he touched her. Too easy to forget the years of isolation that he had helped to cause.

But, did he really?

She had always been strange. How many seven-year olds would think a mystical snow leopard twice her size and glowing with a misty light was a safe companion? She had lived with one foot in a dreamworld, only giving enough attention to reality to function. She had wished for him so fervently because she was already alone.

What really angered her is that they could have been together all those years. But if they had been, would they have come together as they had last night? As lovers instead of companions? She had to admit it was unlikely.

By staying away, he came to her as a prospective lover, not a caretaker.

"What would have happened to me if you had taken me with you that night?" she asked, her voice more level.

He winced, lines of strain appearing at the corners of his eyes. "I would have taken you back to the Yuletide Kingdom as tribute. You would have become a servant to the Winter Queen's court. One of my subjects."

Melanie prickled at the thought. The dreams she had built up around the Yule Cat were nothing like the reality that he would have offered her.

"You make it sound so terrible." Snow's low voice startled her. She had almost forgotten he was there with them. "It isn't. We only take children who are unwanted or who aren't cared for."

"I had a family," she said.

"You were a decoration," Snow said, his voice surprisingly gentle.

She flinched as if he'd struck her. It wasn't his words, though, but the truth behind them.

"Had you ever received clothing on Christmas?" he asked. "New clothing just for you. Not ill-fitting hand-me-downs or dresses you hated but that made you look pretty for pictures they could use to appear as a family?"

Her eyes filled with tears, but she tilted her chin up defiantly, blinking them back. "Just because they didn't give me clothes, that doesn't mean they didn't want me."

Snow nodded. "Yeah, they did. But for their own reasons. Their own purposes. I looked into them when I did your background check. It wasn't love or caring. It was all about appearances."

Her eyes cleared for a moment as the tears she'd been fighting spilled down her cheeks. "So you just judge people and take their kids? What gives you the right?"

"We give them a home," North said, his voice so quiet, she almost didn't hear him.

"In a dreary, winter-locked kingdom?" she said. "How is that better?"

"It wasn't always that way." North shook his head, a haunted look entering his features that made her want to reach out to him. She kept her arms tight to her sides. "There used to be seasons. There used to be spring."

"What about him?" She nodded toward Snow. "The Krampus eats naughty children."

Snow let out a disgusted rumble. "Gods, I wish people would stop saying that. The children I help will never get what they need from this world. They are the unwanted who fall onto the path of darkness. I take them to a world of winter, yes, but also one of light." He lifted his hand and a swirl of snow rose from his palm, forming a tiny Christmas tree, covered in lights of every color. "The people of my kingdom were once just like the children I bring as tribute. We guide them and help them find purpose."

She didn't know what to say. She turned to North and said, "Why didn't you take me as tribute then? If you were helping children, why didn't you help *me*?" She hated how small her voice became as she spoke.

"You wrapped me in your blanket, even though you were freezing," he said. "You promised to take care of me. You loved me." He shook his head. "And then I knew that I was a fraud. I told myself I was helping all those children, that they were better off in the Yuletide Kingdom. But when spring left our world, so did love. I didn't know until that moment what we had really lost. I didn't know what it was to be loved. And I couldn't condemn you to a life in that world." His voice cracked with strain as he forced out the next words. "As I had condemned all those other children."

Her heart broke for him. The pain in his words, his face, his bearing. She had been so caught up in how him leaving her behind had affected her and had never thought of what it had done to him. He had mentioned being exiled. Did that mean he could never go back to his home again? And what had happened to his 'subjects' then? The people—grown or otherwise—who he had brought to that land?

"North…" She took a step closer, but he looked away.

"You're right," he said. "The things I've done. How selfish I've been, even now." His eyes glittered in the light and his voice was hoarse. "I'm not worth it."

She closed the space between them and wrapped her arms around him, just as she had that first night when they met. Pressing her face into his chest, she said, "Giving up my life to wait for the Yule Cat wasn't worth it. But you are."

Chapter Eleven

"If you're both done crapping on our kingdom, it's time to go," Snow said.

North would have to smooth things over with his friend later. At the same time, he had meant every word. Melanie was so ready to give up her life for him. He wasn't quite as eager to let go. He would miss his bakery so much, and seeing the crocuses push through the snow in the spring, feeling the warmth of the summer sun and watching the trees turn to orange and gold in the fall.

If he was going to go back—and take Melanie with him as his bride—things had to change. The Queen would want him to resume his duties, but he couldn't go back to just taking children. There had to be a better way. Maybe his love for Melanie and her love for him could be examples to others. The people of the Yuletide Kingdom could have children of their own, if they learned how to love each other.

Winter might be eternal there, but he could fill it with comfort. Hot cocoa and cookies. Stories by the fire, music and song. There was so much to celebrating the winter season that he had learned in the mortal realm. It would be worth anything to keep Melanie safe and happy. He knew that she would only be happy if the others in his domain were as well.

He pulled back from her far enough that he could gaze into her eyes. "Will you come back with me?"

She smiled, her eyes sparking with excitement as she nodded. "Of course."

"Not really a choice," Snow said. "Like you guys were listening at all."

He shook his head and turned his massive back to them, murmuring complaints that turned into an incantation. Lifting his arms, he swirled them in a circle. Snowflakes filled the space he outlined with his hands, growing thicker and broader until it had become an ellipse floating above the floor large enough for him to step through. He moved to the side and gestured toward the vortex.

"After you," he said.

Melanie glanced at North, worry obvious in her features. He nodded, taking her hand in his as he led her to the portal.

"Are you sure about this?" he asked. "Once we're through, there's no coming back."

"I just... I want to be with you," she said.

Snow leaned closer, hovering over the pair. "Again, not a choice," he said, before straightening.

Melanie actually ignored him. North chuckled at the

way Snow's eyebrow arched and the appreciative glint in his gaze.

"That's all I've ever wanted. Having someone special in my life. And this—" Melanie looked him up and down and smiled. "This is so much better than anything I ever dreamed. My very own fairy prince."

"Ugh, I think I'm going to be sick," Snow said. "And it's Fairy *Lord*. Gods. Just jump through the portal before I toss you through."

Melanie laughed and smiled up at Snow. North had never seen the Krampus look taken aback, but his brows were knitted together in confusion and he leaned back, as if trying to put distance between them. He lifted a massive hand to his chest and rubbed the spot above his heart. If North wasn't mistaken, Snow had just received his first taste of love as well.

Maybe this wasn't a terrible thing at all. Melanie was North's very own spring. With her at his side, anything was possible. He pulled her close, wrapping his arm around her waist.

"You ready?" he asked.

She nodded, her smile brightening as she grabbed onto his waist and held tight. He leapt through the portal, holding her close against his chest. Behind them, North sensed Snow jump through the portal. A moment later, it snapped shut. There was no going back.

The cold was worse than he remembered. Melanie

shrieked as they fell through the perpetual midnight sky, surrounded by auroras of deepest green. North pulled her closer, summoning a zephyr to slow their descent. In the mortal realm, it would only have been perceived as a gentle wind. Here, it took the shape of a beautiful horse, translucent as the misty wind and glowing like the auroras around them. She gasped as it galloped beneath them, sweeping them toward the ground at a less intense angle. It set them down right in front of the castle's doors before dissipating into the air.

"What was that?" she asked, breathless.

"One of my servants," North said. "I'm the Lord of the North Wind."

Her eyes widened. "That was really cool."

A huge drift of snow swept past them, the Krampus riding on top of it. He pulled himself to his feet, shaking off the excess snowflakes from his clothes.

"I'm the cool one," he said. "Lord of Endless Snow." He hooked a thumb toward his chest and then pointed a finger at North. "And that was a dick move."

North tried to suppress a grin as Snow pushed the huge double-doors open and stomped into the castle, mumbling, "Zephyr for two. Yeah, Snow can break his own fall and make his way to the castle."

Melanie pressed herself into North's side and said, "I think you hurt his feelings."

"He's just working through some stuff. I've been gone

a long time."

"You went into exile because of me," she said.

North had wondered if she had picked up on that. He nodded, and said, "It didn't turn out to be the hardship I expected. I mean, the first few years were rough, but then I opened the bakery. Bringing all that warmth to people, making them happy through my baking…" He shook his head. "Honestly, it's kind of addictive. Taking care of people."

"And now you're giving up your exile for me," she said.

"That's not a hardship either. You're worth it." He spun her around to face him. "Besides, I'm hoping we can bring some of that warmth to the Yuletide Kingdom."

"Me, too." She gazed up at the castle walls around them. The clear crystal of the outer walls caught and reflected the lights of the auroras beyond while the interior lights radiated an intense white light, glowing from within. "This place is amazing."

A swarm of pixies flew toward them, their sparkling lights bringing an even bigger smile to Melanie's face as she gasped and ran forward. She spun in a circle, surrounded by the pesky things, looking at them as if they were the most miraculous creatures in existence. They plucked at her hair, pulling strands free and wrapping them into curls around their glowing bodies. Melanie laughed with delight.

"What are these?" she gasped. "Are they alive? Do they understand me?"

"Those are pixies." North stifled a growl, wanting nothing more than to swat them away. He figured that would upset Melanie, though. Plus, the little terrors might take it out on her.

"Pixies!" She turned back to the lights still whizzing around her and reached out a hand.

"I wouldn't do that if I were you," North said. If one of them bit her, it would be over. He would crush them all beneath his boots.

"They're just being friendly." She cupped her hands together beneath a pixie that glowed bright gold. "I'd love to be your friend."

The light hovered over her hands for a few moments, then coalesced into the form of a tiny, lithe, androgynous humanoid with huge eyes and fluffy antennae. Its gossamer wings continued to buzz against its back as it landed on her palms, head cocked to the side curiously. Melanie's eyes widened and she gasped, her body held perfectly still as if she were afraid she would scare a swarm of pixies. A mortal.

"You are utterly beautiful," she whispered, her voice filled with awe.

The pixie jerked back, buzzing into the air for a moment.

"I'm sorry, I didn't mean to offend you," Melanie said.

"You're just… amazing."

It hovered near her face, as if scrutinizing her. Perhaps it was looking for signs of deceit. It wouldn't find any from Melanie. She was the most earnest person North had ever met. It was part of what had let her make her way into his heart. He wondered if the pixie had experienced something similar, as it settled back onto her palm, this time dropping to its knees and letting its wings fold against its back as it stared up at her.

"You are precious," Melanie murmured. "Thank you for this time with me."

Even North felt an odd tug on his heart as he watched the pair. He never thought he could have such gentle feelings for a pixie. Melanie had a way about her. She brought tenderness out of people. He should have known she was the same person as the little girl he had met all those years ago. They both had the same warm heart. Would it survive the cold of the Yuletide Kingdom? Would it survive the harsh judgment of his Queen?

There was no more putting it off. North rested his hand on her back and said, "We'd shouldn't keep the Queen waiting. It's time."

Chapter Twelve

Melanie's heart was beating in her throat as they approached a huge archway that led off from one side of the even bigger hall. She felt like she was walking through an incredible movie set. She could scarcely believe it, but she was walking through an actual fairytale. Snow stood by the open arch, his arms crossed over his enormous chest as he scowled at them.

"Took you long enough." He turned and headed into the room.

North urged her to follow, their arms linked. She rested her hand on his elbow as well. She needed to feel like she could grab onto him if she needed. Truth be told, as much as she'd dreamt of something like this, now that she was living it, she was terrified. She had read the original fairytales as well as the modern revisions. The stories had started off incredibly dark. Even the stories about North and Snow had their frightening versions, more sinister ones where the children were taken away to Faerie to be served in a stew, or gobbled up right in their bedrooms.

A shiver raced down her spine as they walked down a long staircase. The cold of the place seeped into her, making her bones ache. She clutched North's arm tighter, remembering the heat from their passion the previous night. The more she thought about him holding her in his arms, the less she felt the cold. She was blushing by the time the stairs opened out into a room the size of an amphitheater. North followed Snow toward one side, where a raised dais dominated. In the center of the dais was a throne, and on that throne had to be the Winter Queen.

Her white-blonde hair was pulled back in a tight bun covered with a web of intricate platinum chains. On her slight frame, she wore a silken dress of blue as pale as a colorless sky. A crown rested on her forehead, spires of platinum set with diamonds as long as Melanie's forearm seemed to be shooting up toward the sky. Her skin was almost bloodless it was so pale, heightening the red of her lips. As cold as the rest of her was, her eyes were large and as green as a lush spring meadow. They were haunted by sadness and shadowed in pain.

Melanie almost let go of North's arm as she took a step forward, wanting to do something for the Queen, to take the burden that weighed so heavily on her heart. The Queen stiffened in her seat, her lips pulling into a deeper frown. North tightened his grip on Melanie's arm, keeping her at his side. He bowed formally and Melanie gave the best curtsey she could manage.

"My Queen," Snow said, bowing low. As he stood, he

gestured toward North and Melanie with a broad sweep of his hand. "As promised, I bring you Lord North and his bride, Melanie of the Mortal Realm."

North was still bowing, so Melanie held her curtsey. Her calves started to twitch, threatening to cramp. Time seemed to creep to a halt as she waited for someone to say or do something. All she could hear was the blood rushing in her ears until the Queen finally spoke.

"Lord North, your bride is infested with pixies," she said.

North finally stood, pulling Melanie along with him. She tried not to wince as she straightened, discretely stretching stiff muscles.

With an incline of his head, North said, "They do seem to be rather taken with her." He placed his hand over hers where she clutched his arm. "As am I."

"Scatter them," the Queen said.

Melanie spoke without thinking. "They're not hurting anything." She snapped her mouth shut as North tensed beside her. Even Snow's eyes widened as he looked between Melanie and the Queen with misgiving. Melanie's stomach clenched and her heart raced even faster.

"They are bothering *me*," the Queen said.

"Majesty." North nodded, then half-turned toward Melanie.

A cold breeze lifted her hair. She felt the pull of tiny hands holding on, and reached up to gently loosen them, trying to give the pixies a reassuring caress as they were swept away. She did her best to hide her anger, lowering her eyes to the floor. Whatever else this Queen was, she was a bully. Melanie couldn't stand bullies.

"You do not like having those who place themselves in your service being removed from your side?" the Queen said.

"What?" Melanie's gaze snapped up at that. "They aren't my servants, they're my friends."

"Oh, are they?" The Queen angled her head at Melanie, then rose to her feet. She was taller than Melanie realized, the crown adding even more to her imposing height. "You have been in my kingdom for only a few minutes, and already you claim them as friends?"

"I don't claim anyone," Melanie said. "That's not what friendship is about."

North hissed in a breath, his grip on her hand becoming almost painful. Melanie had a feeling she was not making a friend of the Queen. Then again, she wasn't sure she wanted to.

The Queen shook her head as she stepped closer, her movements as smooth as if she were skating across ice. "You poor thing. If only North had brought you to me as a child." Her voice hardened as she said, "I could have taught you proper manners."

Melanie opened her mouth to respond, but a warning squeeze from North helped her hold in her comment.

"I see now that I was wrong to think that a mortal could have a place among us as caretakers of this land." The Queen glanced at Snow and said, "Take her to the servants' quarters. Lord North and I have important matters to discuss."

Melanie's heart felt as if it was about to jump out of her chest. Was she going to be separated from North? Would they ever be allowed to be together again? The room felt like it was spinning as she contemplated an existence in this cold world without him near to warm her heart.

"What?" North pulled her closer against his side and she knew that if they tried to take her away, it wouldn't be without a fight.

"Majesty." Snow surprised her by stepping forward. "This was not the arrangement. Melanie is North's bride. It is done."

"The gaes binds you, too, my Queen." North said, a low growl tracing his words. "Your spell was clear. I was to bring Melanie back as a servant *or* as my bride. I have brought her as my bride."

"She is a disruption," the Queen said. "She has already cost me twenty years' service of one of my most trusted Lords, not to mention the tribute that you would have brought in that time. Do you know how long it has been since the North Wind has carried children to this land? There are so many that we could have aided while you selfishly chased this girl."

Melanie knew that North felt guilty about enjoying his time in the mortal realm. She wasn't about to let the Queen use that guilt against him.

"You are the one who sent him there," Melanie said. "If you want to be angry with anyone, be mad at yourself."

Snow's eyes widened as he stared at her. A slight tremble shook North's body. That was probably not the best thing to say, but Melanie was not going to stand by while someone hurt the man she loved. She stepped closer to him, straightening her spine and raising her chin as she stared defiantly at the Queen.

"Such insolence," the Queen said. "She cannot stay. Remove her from my kingdom."

"Majesty," North bowed.

"Not you." She gestured toward Snow. "The Krampus shall take her back to the mortal realm."

"She is my bride—my mate," North said, wrapping his arms around her. Melanie clung to his side when she had to release his arm. "Wherever she goes, whatever fate befalls her, it's mine to share as well."

"Fine, then you can both go to the servants' quarters," the Queen said. "You will stay there, Lord North, until you learn that mortal love does not last."

Melanie wanted to take her to task for that sweeping statement, but she was too busy worrying about North. She knew she could make the best of whatever the servants' quarters were like. She'd been in bad situations before.

But she wasn't sure if North could stand it. Maybe if he could serve by cooking or baking, he could find some glimpse of happiness, but he would still be trapped in a world he hadn't wanted to return to. After meeting the Winter Queen, Melanie could see why.

"My Queen, please." Snow stepped between the Queen and North. His voice was pleading. "We need him."

"Do we?" She scoffed. "We have functioned well without him all these years. His subjects are grown and his seneschals well trained. They can run his domain with or without him."

"But his duties as Lord of the North Wind—" Snow began.

She cut him off. "Can be handled by Frost."

Snow recoiled. "Frost? *Jack* Frost? He's an insufferable di—"

"He is loyal to me," the Queen said. "As North should have been."

North seemed frozen in place beside Melanie. He stared straight ahead at nothing, a muscle in his jaw twitching.

"Please, I didn't mean to cause any trouble," Melanie said.

"It's rather late for that, don't you think?" the Queen said. "You have been causing trouble for me since you were a child."

"I only wanted to love him," Melanie said. "To care for

him. You can't punish him for that." Dread flooded her as she realized that she had once more spoken out of turn—and that this being was quite possibly the most powerful person she'd ever encountered.

The Winter Queen drew herself up to her full height. Ice and snow gathered in a swirling cloud above them. Freezing rain pelted Melanie, stinging her skin wherever it was exposed. North pulled her against his chest, wrapping his arms around her to shield her from the cold just as she'd done for him the first night they had met. A drift of snow began to form around her and North, quickly rising past their knees. Her teeth chattered and her body shook from the cold.

"I am the Winter Queen," the Queen said. "This is my domain and I will do as I wish."

Melanie was sick of her crap. She shouted over the growing maelstrom so that the Queen would hear her words. "North told me this was a place of safe harbor for children who needed a home. You said you wanted to help me as a child, but now you're fine with hurting me as an adult? Is that your idea of a better place than the mortal realm?"

"My Queen, please." Snow trudged toward them, lifting the fur cloak over Melanie to shield her from the worst of the biting wind.

"North must recommit to me," the Queen shouted. "I will not lose another."

Melanie felt North's chest expand as if he were about to speak. Was he going to offer himself back to the Queen to save Melanie? He would be doomed to remain in this winter land forever, without Melanie at his side to warm him. She couldn't let that happen.

She reached up and grabbed his face, then pulled him down for a kiss. His skin warmed hers, his love flooding into her as he deepened their embrace. She kissed her way to his ear and said, "Whatever fate is mine you will share and I will share yours. I won't leave you here alone."

He claimed her lips again, kissing her so passionately, the cold around her vanished. When he finally pulled back, she saw that the maelstrom had ended. The floor and air around them was clear. The Queen stood several feet away, anguish twisting her features. She schooled her expression, folding her hands before her.

"So be it," she said. "Your fates will be shared. North. You are Lord of the North Wind no more. You will live out your pitifully short life in the mortal realm—as a mortal." She gestured toward Snow, and said, "See to it."

Snow's mouth hung open and his eyes were wide as he stared back and forth between the Queen and North. Finally, he clamped his mouth shut and nodded.

"As you command," he said.

Chapter Thirteen

North felt Melanie tense beside him. He bowed low enough that he could pull her with him into something like a gesture of respect, then immediately stood and headed for the stairs. He glanced down at her, hoping she would see the urgency in his gaze. She started to speak, but he shook his head as discreetly as he could, squeezing her arm again. Her lips tightened into a thin line as she straightened and fell in step beside him. They made their way from the throne room as quickly as he dared. He could hear Snow's sullen footsteps behind them.

North's chest hurt from how long he held each breath. At any moment, the Winter Queen could change her mind and order them to return. He wouldn't be able to relax until they were in the mortal realm. Melanie also seemed to be holding her breath, but he thought it might be more that she was keeping back her words. That was absolutely for the best. He would have to thank her for trusting him when they were safe. Or at least, safer than they were in the Yuletide Kingdom.

As soon as they exited the castle, Snow made a portal again. North didn't hesitate a moment once it was formed.

He lifted Melanie from her feet, holding her tight against his side, and leapt through. They landed in his bedroom on the very spot where they had left. He guided her away from the portal as Snow leapt through, landing heavily on the floor.

The moment the portal snapped shut, Snow let out a huge roar. The glass in the pictures on the wall nearest him cracked from the sound. North kept Melanie clutched against him as she pressed her hands over her ears.

"This is bullshit," Snow bellowed. "We did as we were told. She was supposed to—"

"Snow, please." North reached out and grabbed Snow's arm, hoping to calm his friend before he said something that could get him in trouble, too.

"She's overstepping," Snow said. "She doesn't have the right to transform you into a mortal."

Keeping his voice soft, North said, "I gave her that right when I pledged myself to her."

"No." Snow shook his head fiercely. "No, this isn't right."

"Listen to me." North squeezed Snow's arm. "I'm okay with it. I *want* this."

"But he's right," Melanie said, still rubbing her ears. "She's being unfair and a jerk."

North chuckled darkly. "You've read the lore. Fairness isn't part of the Faerie realm. We were lucky she let us go."

"Only to make an example out of you," Melanie said.

"It doesn't matter why." He wrapped his arms around her and kissed the top of her head. "A mortal life with you sounds wonderful. I wouldn't want to go on forever without you."

"North…" She reached up and stroked his cheek, her fingertips light as the wind.

He grasped her hand and pressed a kiss into her palm, then turned back to Snow. North had never seen such a fierce frown on Snow's face. His brow was knitted tightly, deep furrows between them, and the huge muscles along his jaw flexed and jumped as he ground his teeth together. His hands were clenched in such tight fists, North was afraid he'd draw blood.

"North…" Snow said.

"It's okay." He stepped away from Melanie and nodded. "I'm ready. Do it."

Snow's upper lip curled back from his teeth. He lowered his head and shook it. For a moment, North thought that meant he was going to defy the Queen. That wouldn't end well for any of them. But then, Snow suddenly snapped his head up, his arms stretching wide as he pulled on North's power. North's clothing whipped against his skin as a gale blew forth from him, the intense cold making his bones ache. He had never felt the cold of the North Wind before. But then, he was no longer its master as Snow drew the power into himself.

North staggered as the last bit of it left him. Melanie jumped forward to help catch him, as did Snow. Her warmth comforted him, but there was something more. Something that remained.

"Snow—" North began.

Snow cut him off with a sharp shake of his head. "You are no longer Lord of the North Wind, as my Queen has commanded. I took back what *she* gave to you."

He angled his head for a moment, as if willing North to understand the full meaning contained in his words. North didn't need an explanation. He could feel it. The Yule Cat was still within him. The backs of his eyes burned at the gift his friend had left him, though he didn't know how he could handle being immortal while Melanie wasn't. Snow grabbed North's shoulders and pulled him into a hug that enveloped him. He pressed his cheek against the top of North's head.

"We are as we always were," Snow whispered. "As we always will be, brother. I'm not giving up on you."

North's throat was too tight to speak. He nodded against his friend's chest. Snow gave him a last bone-crushing squeeze and stepped back, releasing him. He summoned another portal, a mix of wind joining his snow. North felt only the slightest pang of loss. He wasn't the Lord of the North Wind anymore, but he was still the Yule Cat, as he always had been and always would be, as Snow had said.

Snow pointed at Melanie and said, "You promised to take care of him and love him forever on that first night when he came to you. I'm going to hold you to that."

"I will." She stepped back to North's side and wrapped her arm around his waist. He draped his arm over her shoulders and hugged her close.

Snow nodded. "Keep the outfits. You might need them later. Merry Christmas."

"Merry Christmas," North and Melanie said together.

Snow stepped through the portal and it snapped shut behind him. They were alone once more. Melanie stood next to North, quietly holding him for several moments.

Finally, she said, "Are you okay?"

North turned to her and smiled. "I'm better than okay. I get to be with the woman I love."

Her eyes widened and she smiled back at him. "I love you, too."

"I know." He smirked and said, "You told me the night we met."

She laughed, stepping closer so that her chest pressed against his. He bent down and claimed her lips gently at first, but then deepening into a long, sensual kiss. She was breathless when they parted.

He left their foreheads touching and said, "Keep telling me."

"Every day," she whispered. "I love you."

"I love you, too. Forever."

He kissed her again, the need to feel her close overwhelming him. They were wearing too many clothes —she was especially. He reached toward the laces of her bodice just as the bell in the shop downstairs rang. Breaking off their kiss, they looked at each other.

"Isn't it still Christmas Day?" Melanie asked. "Are you even open?"

"No, and I locked the door after you came in last night."

"We should see who it is. Maybe they need help."

North took her hands and walked backwards toward the door, pulling her after him. "Maybe they need cookies."

They both laughed as he turned so they could walk through his home together. *Their* home now. He went first down the stairs just in case whoever had arrived wasn't friendly. He had a feeling they were, though. Warmth and happiness coursed through him, even stronger than what he felt when he was with Melanie. He glanced over at her, and from the rosy flush of her cheeks and the bright smile on her face, she felt the same way. There was magic at work that he hadn't experienced before. Magic that he liked.

At the bottom of the stairs, they surveyed the room. Snow was piled up against the door, and the locks were still in place. What had set off the little bell above the door, then? Movement near the tree caught his eye. They turned, and North's breath caught in his chest, his stomach doing flips. A man was bent near the tree, pulling packages from a sack in his hand. He wore dark red jeans with black boots peeking out beneath them and a red jacket. White hair dusted his shoulders as he rose and turned to face them. His cheeks and jaw were covered in a thick snow-white beard.

Melanie made a bunch of odd half-choked sounds, then bellowed, "Santa?"

He laughed and smiled at them, the skin around his eyes crinkling. The warmth North had felt grew a thousandfold. It was almost enough to calm his nerves. Melanie gasped and stepped forward. North couldn't bring himself to move to stop her.

"You're real?" Melanie asked.

Kringle angled his head to the side as he gestured toward North. "What, you believe in the Yule Cat but not Santa?" He laughed again.

"I didn't even think of that," Melanie said. "But… But…"

She looked back and forth between North and Kringle, her brow furrowing. She stepped closer to North and took his hand, her face flooded with concern. It was enough to snap North out of his shock. He placed his hand over his chest and bowed.

"Lord Kringle," North said.

"Oh, please." Kringle winced and shook his head, waving at the air as if trying to dissipate the title. He smiled again, and said, "Call me Kris. Or, Kringle, if you must. I always liked 'Father Christmas,' too." He let out a big chuckle, and said, "Hey, you can call me 'Dad.'"

North sucked in a breath that went wrong and set him into a fit of coughing. Melanie patted his back, still holding onto him with her other hand. He had a viselike grip on her. He was terrified to let go. Kringle was second only to the Winter Queen in power in the Yuletide Kingdom. They were forbidden from speaking of him as he was left to his own work in the farthest reaches of their domain. The only place that still held warmth.

"How about Kringle?" Melanie said. "I think we'd all be comfortable with that."

Kringle chuckled and shrugged one shoulder. "Fine with me."

"May I ask why you're here?" Melanie asked, her earlier wonder replaced with caution.

"I heard about your visit to our kingdom," Kringle said. "I just thought I'd pop in and check on you both. Make sure you're okay."

North felt his eyes grow wide as his eyebrows hitched up his forehead. Was Kringle making a play for North so soon after the Winter Queen cut him loose? What use did he have for the Yule Cat, though? Kringle was all about the joy and giving of the season. North was about consequences—and redemption. Was this his chance to be redeemed?

"I think we're okay." Melanie looked up at North, a question in her expression. He nodded and she smiled.

"Yeah," North said.

Melanie's eyes suddenly widened, and she said, "Cookies! We never finished those cookies." She smiled a bit sheepishly, and said, "You know... Because 'Santa.' Unless that's not—"

Kringle lifted a hand in a reassuring gesture. "I would love some of North's cookies."

"There are plenty in the fridges." North nodded toward the door to the kitchen. "Would you mind grabbing some?"

"Sure." Melanie glanced between the two of them, then hurried from the room.

Kringle looked around, and said, "This really is wonderful. You've created so much joy here."

"I... I suppose," North said. "I just wanted to make it feel like home."

"And you did." Kringle laughed softly as he stepped a bit closer. "You made it feel like home for many, many people."

North hadn't really thought about that when he'd designed the place. He'd wanted it to be as comfortable as possible for himself. If others enjoyed it, too, that was just a bonus.

"I wasn't really trying to make a place for others," North said.

"But you did," Kringle said. "Good deeds don't have to be done consciously for them to bring more joy into the world. You did it without even trying. I wonder what you could accomplish if you actually set your mind to helping." He winked at North and turned back to one of the shelves, staring at an ornate sculpture of a snowflake.

Was he trying to recruit North to his section of the Yuletide Kingdom? North wasn't sure how he felt about that. He had only just gained his freedom from the Winter Queen. Maybe Kringle felt some sort of bond with North now that he had also been removed from her inner circle. But the Winter Queen hadn't taken away Kringle's title. She had left him be in his corner of her Kingdom, free to continue to use his powers as he pleased.

Melanie returned with a big tray full of cookies and three large glasses of milk. North would have to wait to ask any more questions. It was probably for the best, since he needed to sort his thoughts. He would talk to Melanie as soon as Kringle left and get her insight. As Snow kept saying, she had studied the lore.

"Oh, that looks delightful," Kringle said, beaming at her as he picked up a sugar cookie shaped like a bell along with the milk. He took a bite of the cookie and closed his eyes, making happy sounds as he chewed. Melanie kept staring at him as he did. He dusted some crumbs from his beard when he'd finished it.

"Sorry about that," he said. "Hazards of the job."

She smiled and actually giggled, then blushed and pinched her mouth shut. North would have to explain that Kringle had that effect on people, too. He brought out the child in everyone. He also brought out their best. What would it be like to work with him? Not as a subject, but as a colleague? North wondered if that could happen. With Kringle as an ally, anything seemed possible.

Chapter Fourteen

"I can't believe you stopped by on Christmas Day," Melanie said. "Aren't you incredibly busy?"

He shook his head and smiled at her. *Santa* smiled at her.

"That was last night," he said. "Christmas Day is when we all get to relax and spend the day celebrating all we've accomplished. Which reminds me, I should be heading back. But first, if you don't mind..."

He lifted the tray from Melanie's hands and set it aside on a nearby table, then reached into the big pockets in his jacket. He pulled out two perfectly wrapped gifts—one in gleaming gold and the other sparkling blue paper. The gold he handed to Melanie and the blue to North.

"What is this?" North asked.

He had seemed withdrawn ever since Santa arrived. Was there some kind of rivalry going on there between Santa and the Winter Queen? Melanie knew who she would side with, especially after how mean the Winter Queen had been.

"They're gifts." Santa gestured toward them and said, "Open them."

Melanie beamed at North, then lifted her box to her ear and started to shake it. It made a little squeaking sound. Was there a mouse in there? Santa reached out quickly and gripped her arm, stilling it.

"Um… I wouldn't shake that one," he said, winking at her.

Melanie tried to stifle her smile. Santa was touching her arm! She carefully tore through the paper. A beautiful wooden box was inside, ornately carved with an image of the Yule Cat on it.

"Oh look, it's you!" she said, holding it up for North to see. She pulled her lower lip between her teeth and opened the box. A bolt of golden light burst out of it as she did, spinning around her head before landing on her shoulder in its humanish form.

"My pixie friend!" she shouted. "Oh my God, how did you…"

Santa lifted a finger to his lips, and said, "Christmas secrets," then winked at her.

She grinned and nodded. She couldn't believe that she was standing there having a conversation with Santa on the best Christmas Day ever. Melanie set down the box, then lifted a cookie from the tray and offered it to the tiny pixie on her shoulder. Did pixies need to eat? How would she know how to take care of it? The idea of a pixie on a sugar rush didn't seem wise, but by the time Melanie had that thought, the little fairy had already grabbed the cookie from her hand and was happily chomping on it.

North would help her. Together, they would figure everything out. Melanie was more certain of that now than ever. After all, Santa had come to visit them. They were friends now. Her stomach did happy flips as she thought of how amazing her life had become in such a short time. She smiled at North, but he didn't return it. He was staring at the present in his hands.

"You should maybe open that one after I leave," Santa said. He glanced at the tray of cookies and said, "Wedding cookies. My wife always loved these." He looked up to North, his warmth subdued, and said, "Do you mind?"

"Not at all." North gestured toward the pile of cookies. "Take the whole plate."

"One is plenty." Santa patted his surprisingly flat stomach and chuckled as he winked at Melanie again. "I don't want to embody the stereotype." He lifted the cookie and held it, a soft smile pulling at his beard. He tucked the cookie into his pocket and said, "Well, Merry Christmas to you both. If you need anything, just drop me a letter in the mail. I'll be sure to get it."

Melanie felt her eyes grow wide. Santa could get mail? Of course he could get mail. Had he read all the cards she'd sent him as a child? Was he the one who had sent the Yule Cat to her when she'd asked for a kitty over and over again?

A million questions—as well as some squees of joy—

bubbled up inside her. She pinched her lips between her teeth and clutched her hands in front of her chest to keep them from bursting out. Santa just laughed, then walked over to the fireplace.

"I'll see myself out." He placed his finger next to his nose, then burst into a million motes of golden light that swirled up the chimney and were gone.

Melanie couldn't hold it in any more. She practically shouted, "Oh. My. God. That was Santa!" She jumped up and down to get out some of her excitement, but stopped when the pixie on her shoulder made a little squeaking sound of protest. "Oh, sorry."

North was still staring at the present. Melanie reached out to him and squeezed his arm.

"Are you okay?" she asked.

"I don't know." He shook his head. "Kringle is the Winter Queen's counterpart in the Yuletide Kingdom. She's still the ruler, but he has an incredible amount of power. For him to come and visit us now… I don't know what it means."

Melanie angled her head to the side. "Maybe it means that he's happy for us. That he wants us to make this work."

North chuckled and nodded. "I suppose that's possible."

"This is the first day of spending the rest of our lives together," she said. "And it's Christmas. Anything is possible."

North finally smiled and nodded. She stepped closer and grasped his wrists, lifting the present closer to his face.

"Go on," she said. "Open it."

"Fine." He peeled apart the paper, revealing another beautiful wooden box. This one had a heart carved into it.

"Aww," Melanie said. "Maybe that's supposed to represent me since my box had a Yule Cat on it?"

"Maybe." North opened the box and gasped, his eyes widening.

"What? What's wrong?"

He shook his head. With trembling fingers, he lifted a small vial from inside the box. It was filled with a swirling silver light. He clasped the glass in his hand and held it close to his chest, closing his eyes as he smiled softly. Whatever was in that vial, it was making him very happy. He opened his eyes, then held the vial out to her.

"It's for you," he said.

She peered at the beautiful light held in the vial. "What is it?"

"Immortality," he said.

Her eyes widened. A moment ago, she had thought anything seemed possible. But this?

"I thought the Krampus made you mortal," she said. "I don't want to be immortal without you, either."

North's eyes widened, then he grabbed her and pulled her in for a deep kiss. The pixie fluttered from her shoulder and squeaked at them angrily. North broke off the kiss and laughed at the little fairy.

"Sorry about that, little fellow," he said. He turned back to Melanie and said, "I just… I've never felt as loved as I do when I'm with you. I want that forever."

"But if you're mortal—"

"I'm not. Snow only took the powers of the North Wind from me—which the Winter Queen gave me when she asked me to join her court. I've always been the Yule Cat. My immortality is my own."

Melanie felt her eyes widen as she realized what it was North was offering her. "Then we can really be together forever."

"If you'll have me."

"Of course, I will!"

North laughed, then lifted her in a huge hug and spun her around. Endless possibilities flowed through her mind. Everything their life together could hold. Magic and adventure, baking, cooking, and making love. Celebrating holidays, inviting Snow for dinner. Maybe having a cup of cocoa with Santa from time to time. North set her back on her feet and claimed her lips in a deep kiss. She wrapped her arms around his shoulders and held on as tight as she could.

The night they met, she had promised to take care of him and love him forever. She would spend every day of the rest of eternity doing just that.

Epilogue

Snow trudged back to the throne room alone. His friend was trapped in the mortal realm, but at least not in mortal form. For once, Snow did not agree with the Winter Queen's judgment. He didn't like how it felt. He dropped to one knee and lowered his head as she regarded him from her throne, hoping to hide the turmoil in his soul.

"Is it done?" she asked.

"He is Lord of the North Wind no more."

Snow hoped she wouldn't see through his evasion. If she did, she didn't mention it. He felt the heavy weight of her gaze on him. She rose from her throne and strode toward him, pausing at the edge of the dais.

"You were commanded to bring the Yule Cat back to us," she said. "You have failed me in that task. His home is with *her* now. We have lost him."

"My Queen…" Snow lifted his eyes to her at last, knowing that the blazing fires of purpose would burn away any evidence that he hadn't done exactly as she asked. "I will find a way to fix this. I promise you. North will be with us again."

"Careful, Krampus," she said, her voice so cold, it

made his skin crawl. She turned back to her throne and sat down, staring at him with an icy glare. "Do not make promises that you cannot keep."

This was North's home. *They* were his family, even if Melanie now was as well. His friend was just confused from living so many years in the mortal realm. Snow would show North that he needed to return to them. Whatever it took, Snow would find a way to bring them all together again. This wasn't just wishful thinking.

Wish...

The word was a seed in his mind, quickly growing into an idea. A plan. *A hunt.*

He rose, his hands curling into fists as he said, "It will be so."

—

Thank you so much for reading *The Yule Cat!* This project came on suddenly and would not let my muse go. Writing it was an absolute delight and I'm so grateful for the chance to share it with you. I adore Melanie and fell in love with North from the very moment he appeared in my mind. And they aren't the only ones in this world who have stolen their way into my heart.

The magic continues in the next book of the trilogy, *The White Stag.* Read on to get an idea of what Krampus is up to as he tries to find a way to bring his best friend out of exile (and don't worry, Krampus's story will finish out the trilogy!)

The White Stag

Court of the Yuletide Fae
Book Two

Chapter One

The lights from the Christmas tree gleamed in rainbow patterns on the cabin walls. Sylvia pulled her blanket closer around her shoulders as she stared at them. She should probably take the decorations down, since it was getting closer to New Year's. But they were a reminder that she had made it through her first Christmas Day as a single woman in years, even if she'd spent it at the same cabin where she and her ex, David, had always celebrated.

He accused her of claiming the cabin out of spite, but she honestly just loved the place. She let him have the house and his fancy car. Thank God they didn't have any kids or pets. All she had really wanted was this cabin and everything in it, and the beautiful forest surrounding it. The nearest neighbor was miles away, which had been a draw at first, but she had to admit, she was getting a little lonely. And cold.

She reluctantly let the blanket fall on the couch, then went to the fire and added a few more logs. While they caught, she hurried upstairs to get more blankets and pillows. This was going to be a night for sleeping in front of the fire, it seemed. She looked out the window in the loft area, barely able to make out the trees through the driving snow in the fading light. They had definitely received their white Christmas—and then some.

She shivered as the cold hit her, then grabbed all the blankets piled on the bed and pulled them into her arms, along with several pillows. She could barely see the stairs as she made her way back downstairs. At least they would cushion her landing if she tripped. When she made it to the fireplace, She dropped them on the plush fake-fur rug in front of the safety screen, then grabbed the poker to stir up the blaze.

Sylvia had just finished banking the fire when a tremendous crash rocked the walls of her cabin. Pictures shook on the walls and the many bookshelves tilted back and forth precariously. She fell backwards, luckily landing on her blanket pile.

"What the heck was that?"

It had almost sounded like an explosion. She quickly

put the poker back in its place and set the fire screen in front of the hearth to keep the blaze she'd worked up in place. She had really been looking forward to cozying up with the pile of blankets and pillows she'd piled in front of it. Hopefully, whatever this was, she'd be able to proceed with her evening as planned.

She ran to the front door and grabbed her coat, hat, and gloves. Even a few minutes outside would freeze her solid, and she wasn't in the mood to turn into a snow person. She pulled everything on in record time, then grabbed her go-bag and hurried outside, shutting the door behind her as quickly as she could to keep the warmth of the cabin inside.

Dusk was spreading over the forest, but she still had enough light to see. The snow falling in thick chunks worried her a lot more than the darkness. She grabbed the emergency sled she kept by the door, just in case she needed it, and headed toward the sound of the crash.

Before too long, evidence of... something began to show around her. The trees above had broken branches and piles of snow beneath where everything that had been stuck to their limbs had been dislodged. It was almost like a meteor had come through.

"That's not good," she said. "Then again, neither is talking to myself constantly." She'd gotten into the habit after staying in the cabin alone for so long.

Maybe she was about to have an encounter with little

green men. As long as there wasn't any probing involved, she'd be fine with making new friends. Heck, if the guy looked like some of the sexy aliens on the covers of some of those Scifi Romances she'd seen at the bookstore last time she went into town, she might not mind a little probing.

"I really have been alone too long."

She checked her GPS to make sure it was still working okay and she could find her way back to the cabin, even after dark, then trudged deeper into the forest. More evidence led the way for her. Whole trees had been felled. Her meteor theory was gaining ground. She skidded down an incline, pausing in a level spot that seemed to be the end of the event horizon.

The light was fading, but she could still see well enough. Even better, the area was slightly shielded from the heavy snow. Scanning the area, all she saw was white snow drifts punctuated by the occasional branch sticking through it. What could have caused all this damage, though? Had it already been covered in snow?

"Well, that was a waste," she said. Hopefully, the fire would still be burning nice and hot when she returned to the cabin. At least it hadn't taken too much time.

A sudden movement in her periphery caught her eye and she froze. It wasn't the wind or snow. One of the branches had moved. She was sure of it. She should just turn around and keep heading back to her cabin and leave things be, but what if it was some animal that had been hurt when whatever this was had happened?

"Dangit." Cautiously, she made her way closer to the branch.

It stirred again as she grew closer. The way the branch had grown didn't look quite right. She wasn't sure what was off about it until she was almost on top of it and saw that it wasn't a branch at all. It was an antler. An antler attached to the biggest, most beautiful stag she had ever seen. If it was a stag.

Its fur was completely white, blending in almost perfectly with the snow covering its body. The antlers caught the light oddly, gleaming almost gold in the fading sun. They were also caught in a bunch of other branches and debris. It almost looked like the poor thing had crashed through the trees.

"Oh boy," she said. "You look like you're in a predicament."

She glanced up at the trees and froze. Standing right next to the stag, she could clearly see a line of damage that led straight to him. But it started at the tops of the trees. It started in the sky, as if *he'd* been the meteor.

"Okay, this is very weird."

She turned back to him and gasped. As the light faded more, she could clearly see that his eyes were glowing, casting a soft gold on the snow in front of him. Weren't there legends about a white stag? Like, if you caught him, he had to grant you a wish? There were so many things Sylvia would wish for. World peace—could he manage that? Happy homes for children and honestly everyone who needed them. Enough money to try to make a difference in the world if he couldn't grant wishes that big.

He let out a sigh, and looked up at her, his eyes filled with so much sadness. Who gave a crap about wishes? This being—whatever he was—needed her help. She had to focus. They had already lost almost all their light.

"Sorry," she said. "This is kind of a new experience for me."

But only kind of. She had rescued animals and even people before. That's why she had the sled. It was big enough for a person, but she wasn't sure about the stag. She started digging out the snow around him, sweeping it away with her gloved hands. The snow darkened as she did. Had he stirred up some dirt as he fell? That didn't make sense. The ground was frozen.

Cautiously, she dusted the snow away from his body. She hissed in a breath as she saw four long gashes marring his white fur from his neck down to his shoulder. They weren't bleeding anymore, but they looked painful and deep. She reached out to gingerly touch the skin around the area. The stag didn't flinch, but he watched her with wary eyes.

"I promise I won't hurt you," she said. She peered more closely at the injury. "What did you face off with? A giant grizzly?"

The stag closed his eyes, his head lowering as much as it could with all the debris locked amongst his antlers. How was she ever going to get him out of this? Now that she had cleared some of the snow from around him, she could see a large branch that was way too heavy for her to move—and the snow was still coming down. She would need a chainsaw to get him out of this and a tent or awning to keep the area clear while she worked. Even if she did get him free, he wouldn't fit on her sled. He was at least twice the size of any stag she'd ever seen.

"I don't know what to do," she said, resting one hand on his chest and the other on his antlers. "You're so tangled up, it'll take me hours to free you. Not that I'm not going to try," she quickly added. "I won't give up on you. I just… I wish I could help you better."

The antler she was holding onto warmed against her glove. She gasped and tried to pull away, but her hand was frozen in place. Not from the cold, but from something else. The antler glowed bright gold, the light spreading over the stag and illuminating his entire body. He put off so much warmth, the snow around them melted.

She squinted against the brightness he was putting off, trying to see what was happening. It looked as though his entire body was turning into pure light. She finally had to close her eyes against it, but she could feel him rippling and shifting under her hands. The antler she was stuck to shrank and flattened, the shape of his chest changed, heaving with quick breaths. She heard him take in a huge gasp, like someone surfacing from water after too long below, and opened her eyes.

The most beautiful man she had ever seen was sprawled before her on the ground. His hair was pitch black, shorter on the sides than the top. Dark stubble coated his jaw. His eyebrows were also dark and strong, resting above thick lashes that surrounded amber-gold eyes. His soft lips were parted as he took in deep breaths.

Her gaze strayed over the rest of him, her eyes widening the more she saw. Broad shoulders and sculpted chest, rows of abs stacked on each other, muscled thighs and in between... Goosebumps raced along her skin, and not because of the cold. In fact, she was starting to feel quite warm—in certain places. Her eyes had to be popping out of her head. He was beyond perfect.

No one can be this hot.

Sylvia shook herself as she noticed four angry red lines that ran from his neck down across one shoulder. His wounds had healed incredibly, but they were still there. Whoever—whatever—this guy was, he needed her help, not for her to be lusting after him. And hadn't he just been a deer? Unless she had hallucinated that whole thing. That would make more sense, but she couldn't bring herself to believe it. No, this guy was some kind of... deer shifter. Yeah, that made sense. Like in the Paranormal Romances she'd been devouring since she arrived at the cabin.

He was a super-hot deer shifter and she was going to slap him on her sled and take her back to her cabin. Where she would be respectful of his boundaries. And not lust after him. Not at all.

'Yeah, good luck with that,' she thought.

—

I'm so thrilled to bring *The Yule Cat* to you and start this journey into a brand new world! The magic continues in the next book of the trilogy, *The White Stag*. You'll find links to many distributors for the book on my website at ***https://cassandra-chandler.com/the-white-stag/***

For more of my Paranormal Romances, check out ***The Summer Park Psychics*** or ***Forbidden Instinct***. If you want to explore my other stories, you can go on out of this world adventures with the fated soulmates of the ***Cygnian 7*** series or check out short, steamy Sci-Fi Romances on a near-future Earth in that same universe with ***The Department of Homeworld Security***. And if you'd like a little bit of Scifi mixed into your Paranormal Romance, check out the ***Blades of Janus***.

I'd love to keep in touch. Join my newsletter at sendfox.com/cassandrachandler to hear about all the adventures happening in Cassland. And if you enjoyed this book, please consider leaving a review at your favorite book review site. Reviews are so important to authors. You can also help by spreading the word among your friends. I appreciate you so much!

Thank you for reading *The Yule Cat,*

Cassandra Chandler

About the Author

USA Today Bestselling author Cassandra Chandler uses her vivid imagination to make the world more interesting, spawning the ideas she turns into her enthralling Science Fiction Romances and darkly evocative Paranormal and Urban Fantasy Romances. Fast-paced and funny, lighthearted or dark, her stories will introduce you to characters you'll fall in love with and worlds you long to explore.